EXEMPLARY ISLAMIC STORIES

EXEMPLARY ISLAMIC STORIES

By

Mian Obaid Ali Shah

Hinge Publishers
London

 Hinge Publishers

First published in Great Britain in 2022 by Hinge Publishers

Publisher's note

Hinge Publishers believes that information in the book is accurate and reliable at the time of publication, and every effort has been made to ensure the accuracy of the text. Hinge Publisher, the authors and the contributors accept no responsibility for inaccuracies whatsoever for consequences that may arise from errors, omissions, opinions, suggestions, advice, etc., given in the book.

ISBN 978-1-7396556-0-0

Contents

Table of Contents

Almighty Allah

Role Models

Friendship

Education

Contents

Contents

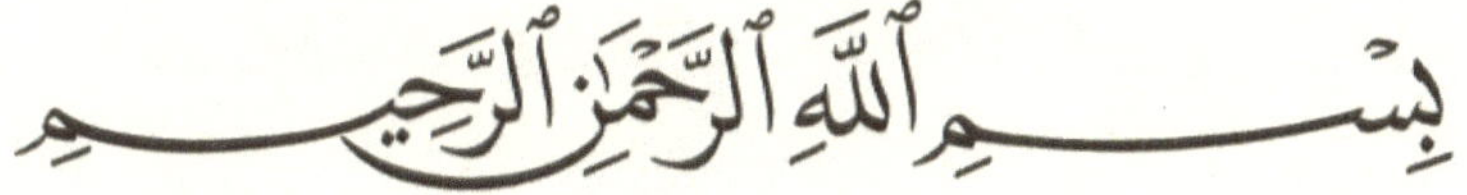

In the name of Allah, The Most Gracious and The Most Merciful

Foreword I - Zafar Iqbal

Stories, anecdotes and parables are highly effective ways of conveying a message. They can improve our understanding and empathy. Storytelling is a powerful tool for teaching because it gets us near to realities and provides us with a near real-life predictable experience. Stories, particularly true stories, trigger our imaginations and motivate us by touching our emotions.

The Noble Quran and Hadith also contain inspiring stories. These narratives teach us vital lessons about important issues we face in our everyday lives. Our Imams in mosques often tell Islamic stories as a part of their Friday sermons. Some stories we keep hearing regularly. The repetition of the same story helps attract people's attention and urges us to give them significant consideration. Repeating something, again and again, helps get engraved in the heart and mind and leads to acceptance and actions.

Alhamdulillah, the writer has done marvellous work by compiling some wonderful authentic exemplary Islamic stories. The selected stories encompass all walks of our lives. They set a clear direction for the readers to follow. Every story in the book carries a lesson and, if followed properly, could be like a lighthouse showing the path towards success in this world and the Hereafter as well.

I hope that the book will serve its real purpose of acquainting readers, especially our young generation, with true Islamic values and revitalising their moral standards. Teachers and parents can also add the book to their advisory toolkit to be used in providing guidance.

Zafar Iqbal
Imam Madina Masjid Levenshulme
Manchester, United Kingdom
March 2022

Foreword II – Qasim Swati

The book, Exemplary Islamic Stories, is a collection of tales, narratives, accounts and records derived from the Holy Quran, Hadiths and other Islamic books about how to live our lives as instructed by Islam. Stories are said to be the best teachers and a wonderful source of learning for humans.

We all need and love stories for certain reasons. Whether this is in the shape of a novel, fable, a description of real-life events or any other form, we need to read and listen to stories that can provide us with forces responsible for our physical and mental growth and wellbeing.

The current book is a great teacher both for children as well as adults for improving their spiritual and mental performance. Especially, this book can hugely prove helpful for the mental growth of the new generation, particularly those who live in the western countries of the globe, as these children need to be taught about how to improve their mental and spiritual capacity.

That is why a famous African-American social reformer, writer, orator, abolitionist and statesman, Frederick Douglass (1818-1895), once said, as: "It is easier to build strong children than to repair broken men."

Thus, it is hoped that this book can benefit not only adults but can be very useful, particularly for children, to learn from it and shape their lives in a way expected from them by Islam, in particular, and humanity, in general.

Qasim Swati
Freelance Journalist, Writer and Human Rights Activist
United Kingdom
Qasimswati.com
March 2022

Preface

The primary purpose of this book is to make our young Muslim generation aware, especially those who live in western countries, of what real success in this world is. Today, people spend time and money on attending events and training courses to get inspired and motivated. They sit down and listen to the motivational speakers and their success stories. Motivation does not come from the outside but from the inside instead. Unless the inside is not ready, it is impossible to get motivated.

Conveying a message in the form of a story is a compelling way of learning and understanding. It helps readers to understand complex issues efficiently. Even in the Holy Quran and Hadith, a fair portion of the teachings consists of stories. The essence of writing this book is to motivate our young generation through the real-life stories of our elders.

This book can also be very effective for adults struggling to control their anger and want to suppress their greed or facing some other issues in life.

The book comprises over fifty stories on different topics, which have been shortlisted after going through hundreds of books. The following key aspects have been considered to ensure authority and authenticity in the book:

- The use of authentic sources;

- When required, minimal changes in wording for better readability and comprehension, but ensuring that the core and crux of the story remain unchanged;
- Provided explanations in footnotes.

I would like to thank those who supported me through their comments, feedback and reviews. Their efforts and assistance have formed the foundation of this book.

I would like to pay special thanks to Qasim Swati for his crucial feedback and editorial support. He provided many valuable comments, which were incorporated into the book. I am also obliged to Zafar Iqbal (Imam of Madina Masjid in Manchester, UK) for his encouragement.

Special thanks also go to our young readers, especially my son Mian Muhammad Abdulhadi, whose inquisitive mind inspired me to embark on writing this book. He was the first person who finished the book manuscript before anyone else and provided constructive feedback. Other early readers of the book included Maya, Zara, Rafael, Zoya, Yusaf and Adan.

From the core of my heart, I pray that may Allah protect and give long life to all those who contributed to this book directly or indirectly. May Allah also raise the status of those authors whose books I consulted during my research.

Finally, may Allah show the right path and give success in this world and the Hereafter to all those who read the book for seeking guidance.

Special Note

I request all the readers to kindly send their valuable feedback and suggestions to me (the author) at obaidshah78@gmail.com.

Any proceeds (profit) from the sale of this book will be donated to poor living in extreme poverty in Pakistan.

Organisations which want to independently print and distribute this book for non-profit purpose, please contact the author directly at obaidshah78@gmail.com.

Mian Obaid Ali Shah
London
March 2022

The Existence of Allah

One day, an atheist (Someone who does not believe in God) challenged the Muslims to prove the existence of God. When the king heard about it, he asked Imam Abu Hanifa (Rah[1]) to come and debate with the atheist. Imam Abu Hanifa[2] accepted the debate and said that he would be there on the fixed date and time.

People started gathering to watch the debate as the time approached. The debate was supposed to begin anytime, but there was no sign of Imam Abu Hanifa. Then it was getting late, and everyone was waiting for the Imam.

Meanwhile, the atheist started complaining, "If your debater can not keep his promise, how he can win the debate? Probably he is scared and has no answers. That is why he did not show up."

At last, Imam Abu Hanifa arrived. The king welcomed him and seated him near his throne.

The atheist demanded, "Tell me, why were you so late?"

Imam Abu Hanifa said, "My home is on the other side of the River Tigris (Dajla). I needed a boat to cross it. So I waited there for a boat to come, but none came. As I was waiting by the river, I saw a tree nearby falling down. It started chopping itself neatly into logs. Then, the logs shaped themselves into planks, nailed to each other, and turned into a boat. When I boarded it, it sped me across the river to the city."

The atheist started laughing and said, "I had heard that you are the most knowledgeable person among the Muslims. But what you just said is a white lie. No one would ever believe this lie."

The Imam asked, "So, you think I am making this up?"

The atheist yelled, "Of course! I don't believe a single word of what you just said."

Then Imam Abu Hanifa concluded, "If you cannot accept that a simple boat can create and operate itself, how can you believe that our entire universe came into existence by itself and run by itself?"

By hearing the Imam's allegorical argument, the atheist was speechless and had no answer to the questions of the Imam.

*****

Once a Roman came to Baghdad and asked Khalifah (Caliph/ruler) Mansoor, "I have three questions and is there anyone in your kingdom who can accept the challenge of answering them?"

Khalifah agreed to the challenge and invited all renowned scholars in his court, including Imam Abu Hanifa.

At the start of the debate, the Roman sat upon the pulpit (Mimbar[3]) and raised his questions:

My first question is: "What was there before Allah?"

My second question is: "Which direction is Allah facing?"

My last question is: "What is Allah doing at this moment?"

When people heard these questions, they got silent, and no one came up with satisfactory answers.

At that time, Imam Abu Hanifa came forward and said, "I will answer all three questions. But my condition is that you have to come down from the pulpit."

The Roman stepped down, and Imam Abu Hanifa sat on the pulpit.

Imam Abu Hanifa then asked the Roman to ask the questions again.

The Roman asked, "What was there before Allah?"

Imam Abu Hanifa replied, "You are able to count, so please, can you count the numbers?"

When the Roman started counting from figure one, Imam asked him to start before one.

The Roman argued, "There is nothing before one. The first numeral is one."

Imam Abu Hanifa declared, "Exactly the same way Allah is also one, and there is no one before Him."

The Roman then asked his second question, "Which direction is Allah facing?"

Imam Abu Hanifa requested a candle and asked the Roman, "Tell me, in which direction does the candle's light face?"

The Roman replied, "In all directions."

Imam Abu Hanifa answered, "Allah also faces in all directions."

The almost defeated the Roman gathered his courage and asked the third question, hoping to make the Imam answerless this time, "What is Allah doing at this moment?"

Imam Abu Hanifa answered, "Amongst other things that Allah is carrying out at this moment, he brought you down the pulpit and elevated me above you."

Answering these questions, the Roman became silent and bowed his head in defeat.

*****

Hazrat[4] Imam Razi (Rah) was a great Islamic scholar, an expert on the Holy Quran's exegesis, Muhaddith (scholar of Hadith[5]) and a great Islamic researcher. When he completed his Islamic education, he planned to learn about his 'self' (nafs[6]). For that purpose, he started searching for a saint. He tried a lot, and eventually, he found his spiritual teacher who could help him. Imam Razi requested to accept him in his allegiance (Bayat) for spiritual education. First, the great saint refused his request, but on Imam Razi's insistence, the saint inducted him into his students and took a religious pledge from him.

Imam Razi continued his education and learned invaluable knowledge from his spiritual teacher. At that time, atheism was at its peak. Atheists do not believe in the existence of God. They were challenging scholars to prove the existence of God through logic and arguments. Imam Razi had one hundred arguments for proving the existence of Allah. He usually could beat atheists in the first fifteen arguments whenever he debated (Manazra) with them.

When Imam Razi was on his deathbed, Satan came to him humanly and sat near his head. He tried to misguide him about the existence of Allah.

Satan asked him about Allah's existence. Imam said, "Of course, Allah does exist."

Satan asked him to provide any proof in support of his belief in the existence of Allah.

Imam Razi gave him a logical reason, but Satan dismissed that with a counter-argument. Imam gave him another reason, which Satan thwarted. Imam Razi gave reason after reason, but the stranger (Satan) was so good at reasoning and always provided a counter-argument. When Imam Razi gave seventy reasons in support of the existence of Allah and Satan foiled all of them, the Imam started worrying.

Imam Razi wondered who that person was, who almost defeated him. Imam Razi became so worried that if that stranger were smashing all his arguments with such a speed, then all his hundred arguments would finish and then eventually, he may also technically doubt the existence of Allah. That means that he would die as an atheist and end up in Hell.

He was so worried about what to do because the defeat in this debate meant his destination would be in Hell as it was his death time. When he gave his 99th reason in support of the existence of Allah, Satan also falsified his argument. Imam Razi started sweating out of fear on his deathbed.

Imam Razi remained a student of a saint, so his acquaintance came to help. His spiritual teacher discovered Imam Razi's situation miles away. The saint was performing his ablutions (Wudu) at that time, and he smashed his water pot on the ground out of rage and shouted, "Oh Razi, why do not you say that I accept Allah without any logical reason."

Allah communicated these words from his spiritual teacher to Imam Razi seamlessly. When these words reached Imam Razi's ears like a magical whisper, he quickly passed them to the stranger, "I accept the existence of Allah without any logical reason."

When Satan heard these words, he ran away as this argument was unbeatable, as no one can argue against such an assertion.

When Imam Razi reiterated these words, he died, and due to his company with a noble person, he died as a true Muslim (a believer in Islam).

Lesson: Knowledge is power, and it can enable a person to think in a better way. Imam Abu Hanifa was a great and quick-witted scholar. He used to make the opponents speechless by giving them elementary common sense examples.

It is simply common sense that there is Someone, Who created this entire universe and running it. When we see a book, can we imagine is it written, printed and bound by itself? Of course, not. So, if we cannot believe that a simple thing can happen by itself, how can we imagine that the whole universe came into being by itself?

The Fear of Allah

One day, Hazrat Adham (father of a great saint, Hazrat Ibrahim Bin Adham) was going through farms in Bukhara City. On the way, he performed ablutions on the canal bank. Meanwhile, he saw an apple floating in the water, which he picked and ate.

After finishing the apple, a thought came to his mind. He realised that the apple probably had fallen from one of the trees in the farm. He assumed it because the canal was passing through an apple garden.

He realised it was not permissible (halal[7]) to eat something without permission from its owner. He started walking through the canal against the flow of the water to find out where it came from. At last, he found the garden, which he believed to be the one whence the apple had come.

He knocked on the door to see if he could inform the owner about what had happened and asked for forgiveness so that the apple may become permissible for him. After knocking on the door, a girl came out. Hazrat Adham asked her to call the owner of the garden. She told him that the owner of the garden was a woman.

He then asked her, "I want to see her for an important matter." Eventually, he got permission to see the owner and told her the whole story.

She told him, "I own half of the farm while the king (Sultan) owns the other half. Although I forgive my half part of the apple, but see Sultan for the other half."

He was told that Sultan lived in Balkh, which was a ten-day journey. To get forgiveness for the remaining half of the apple, he went to Balkh. When he reached there, he saw the king's procession there. He got the opportunity to talk to him. He told the king the whole story and asked for forgiveness for the remaining part of the apple.

The king said, "I cannot say anything now, but you should come tomorrow to the palace, and I will decide there."

The king had a beautiful daughter. She was pious and God-fearing. The king refused several offers for her marriage as he wanted to marry her to a pious person.

When the king returned to the palace, he told the entire story about Hazrat Adham (Rah) to the daughter. He told her, "I had seen none like him who would come all the way along from Bukhara to Balkh just to make a half apple halal." The daughter accepted her father's offer and agreed to the marriage.

The next day when Hazrat Adham arrived at the palace, the king told him, "I would forgive my half of the apple on one condition if you marry my daughter."

Hazrat Adham kept refusing the offer, but the king insisted that it was the only condition he would forgive his part of the apple. At last, Hazrat Adham agreed to marry his daughter.

The whole palace was well decorated for the wedding. When Hazrat Adham saw his wife, she was gorgeous. After the marriage, the king forgave him for eating the apple.

After a few days, he died on a prayer mat after finishing his prayers. The mother gave birth to a boy named Hazrat Ibrahim bin Adham (Rah). As the king had no sons, so Hazrat Ibrahim bin Adham became the heir to the throne. However, he renounced the throne, chose asceticism, and became famous as a Sufi [8]legend.

Moral: God-fearing people do not do a good thing for personal pleasure. When people follow the true teachings of Islam, they can be successful in both this world and the Hereafter.

Hazrat Sulaiman (AS) and a Fish

It is narrated that once Prophet Sulaiman[9] (AS[10]) asked an ant, "What is your sustenance every year?"

The ant replied, "A grain of wheat."

So Hazrat Sulaiman (PBUH[11]) confined it in a bottle with a grain of wheat. After one year, he saw that the ant ate only half of the food. He inquired the ant why it did not finish the food.

The ant replied, "I relied on Allah prior to my confinement to the bottle, and since I was confined, my reliance remained upon you. I was scared that you would forget me, so I saved half of the grain for the next year."

Hazrat Sulaiman (AS) then asked God to allow him to feed all the animals for one year. Allah revealed to him that he has no such power to do so. Prophet Sulaiman (AS) then asked for a month, which was also declined. He then requested Allah to be allowed to provide food for all the animals for a week, but Allah said, "It is still impossible." Hazrat Sulaiman (AS) then asked for a period of one day. Allah said, "Still, you have no such power, but I will give you permission for one day."

Hazrat Sulaiman (AS) ordered both jinns and humans to prepare a great feast. They gathered a lot of food and then spread them across. The feast was as big as a month's journey in length and width on each side. Allah then asked Hazrat Sulaiman (AS) which animal he wanted to start feeding with.

He replied that he wanted to start it with sea animals. Then Allah ordered a fish from an ocean to go and eat from Prophet Sulaiman's feast. The fish came and ate all the food at once.

The fish said to Hazrat Sulaiman (AS), "I am still hungry."

Hazrat Sulaiman asked, "Is your daily food more than this?"

The fish said, "Much more than this."

Prophet Sulaiman then prostrated to Allah and said, "You are the only One Who can feed all of us."

Lesson: Allah has the power to provide food to all living beings. He has created a giant food supply chain for all types of beings, whether humans, animals, birds or insects. He is responsible for feeding every single living creature.

The Steadfastness of Muhammad (PBUH)

It was the tenth year of the revelation, which is also known as the Year of Grief. Muhammad's (PBUH) wife, Hazrat Khadijah (RA[12]), and his uncle, Abu Talib, had just passed away. After the death of Abu Talib, the Quraysh in Makkah got the opportunity to torture Muslims freely and, therefore, increased their sinister plots against the Prophet (PBUH).

Due to the disobedience and enmity of the people of Makkah, he felt disappointed and started thinking that they would not embrace Islam. Hence, he went to the outskirts of Makkah to preach Islam over there. The Prophet Muhammad (PBUH) took a fifty miles journey from Makkah to Taif to convey the message of Islam.

During his journey to Taif, his slave Hazrat Zayd Bin Haarisah (RA) also accompanied him. At Taif, there lived Banu Thaqif, a clan strong in number. Taif was a city of rich people. The Prophet (PBUH) left for Taif with the hope of winning them over to Islam. When he reached Taif, he visited the three chieftains of the clan separately and invited them to Islam. He called upon them to stand by His Prophet's (PBUH) side.

However, they gave a very blasphemous (disrespectful) reply. They told him that they did not like his stay in their town. The Prophet (PBUH) had expected civil treatment in speech from them, as they were the heads of the clan.

But one of them mocked, "Hey, Allah has made you a Prophet!" The other ridiculed, "Could Allah not find anyone else besides you to make him His Prophet?"

The third one rejected him and said, "I do not want to talk to you, for if you are in fact a Prophet, then to oppose you is to invite trouble, and if you only pretend to be one, why should I talk with an impostor?"

The Prophet (PBUH), who was a rock of steadfastness and perseverance. He did not lose heart over the indecent treatment from the chieftains and tried to approach the common people; but nobody listened to him.

When he realised that further efforts were in vain, he decided to leave the town. But they did not let him depart in peace and set the street urchins after him to hoot and stone him. The vicious gang surrounded and stoned him until his blessed feet were soaked in blood.

Hazrat Zayd Bin Haarisah would run to shield him by standing ahead of and behind him. He himself was also covered in blood and lost control.

When The Prophet (PBUH) was far out of the town and safe from the troublemakers, he prayed to Allah. The prayer made the Heavens move, and Hazrat Jibrail (AS) appeared before the Prophet (PBUH) and said, "Allah knows all that has passed between you and these people.

He has deputed an angel in charge of the mountains to be at your command."

Saying this, Jibrail (AS) ushered the angel before the Prophet (PBUH). The angel greeted the Prophet (PBUH) and said, "O, Prophet of Allah! I am at your service. If you wish, I can cause the mountains overlooking this town on both sides to collide so that all the people therein would be crushed to death, or you may suggest any other punishment for them."

The merciful and noble Prophet (PBUH) said, "Even if these people do not accept Islam, I do hope from Allah that there will be people from among their progeny who would worship Allah and serve His cause."

Lesson: We get irritated over a bit of trouble or abuse from somebody and then we keep on torturing and taking our revenge throughout our lives in every possible manner. After so much suffering at the hands of the Taif's mob, Muhammad (PBUH) neither cursed them nor did he work for any revenge, even when he had the full opportunity to do so. This story has a great lesson about steadfastness, patience, and forgiveness.

The Generosity of Hazrat Ali and Hazrat Fatima

One day, Hazrat Hassan (RA) and Hazrat Hussain (RA), the grandsons of Hazrat Muhammad (PBUH), became very sick. Their mother, Hazrat Fatima (the daughter of Muhammad (PBUH)), promised that she and her husband Hazrat Ali would fast for three consecutive days if both their children got cured.

Soon, Allah recovered the children. The parents then started fasting as per their promise. When the time of iftar (opening fast) came, they had only one bread altogether. By the time they started opening the fast, there was a knock on their door.

When asked, the person said, "I am poor and hungry and came to the door to see if I can get something for eating."

Both husband and wife decided that they could afford to stay hungry but should not return the person empty-handed. They gave their bread to the beggar and opened their fast just by drinking water.

The next day, they fasted again by just drinking water as there was nothing to eat. During the day, Hazrat Ali worked and took the wages just to buy one bread. When the time of iftar came near, there was a knock on the door. When the door opened, an orphan was on the door who asked for food. Both husband and wife gave their bread to the orphan. This time they again opened their fast just by drinking water.

They held the third fast the next day by drinking only water. They brought some food for the iftar, but that time a slave knocked on the door, and they gave their food to him.

Now for three consecutive days, they fasted with only water. They felt weakness. However, they did not return anyone empty-handed from their door when they were asked for food in the name of Allah.

Their love for Allah and His people was unimaginable. They were ready to sacrifice their lives for the pleasure of Allah. Thus, donating their portion of food and remaining hungry was not a big deal for them in order to make Allah pleased.

Lesson: Hazrat Muhammad (PBUH) and his Companions (RA) were role models for us, and we should follow in their footsteps. We should take care of the poor and the needy around us and support them as much as possible. When someone asks us something in the name of Allah, we should support them. After all, whatever we own is also given to us by Allah. When Allah sees that we are generous to the needy people, He will reward us more.

Humbleness and Politeness

Hazrat Umar Ibn Al-Khaṭṭab (RA) was the second Khalifa (leader) in Islam and was known for his piousness and just nature. One day, he went through a narrow street and put his feet on a beggar.

The beggar did not know Hazrat Umar (RA) and voiced angrily, "Are you blind? Do not you walk with open eyes?"

Hazrat Umar (RA) humbly replied, "Brother! I am not blind but made a mistake unintentionally. So, please forgive me for the sake of God."

These were the humble words to the beggar from one of the greatest rulers governing a region spread over hundreds of thousands of square kilometres of land. This was the person who destroyed the Qaiser-o-Kisra's (Caesar and Khosrow) kingdoms. Allah's enemies were so sacred of hearing about Hazrat Umar that their knees would weaken, and their hearts would tremble to hear about his name.

Satan had also given up on Umar. The Prophet Muhammad said[13], "O son of Khattab, by the One in Whose Hand is my soul, whenever Satan sees you taking a path, then he will take another path."

*****

Hazrat Ibrahim bin Adham (Rah) was born as heir to the king, but he abandoned the throne to become an ascetic (Sufi). One day he was on his way when a drunken young man riding a horse came to him, lashed him, and said, "Carry this wine jar on your head to my place."

Ibrahim bin Adham carried the jar on his head and took it to the person's home." When he got there, he saw a singer was playing the sarangi (a musical instrument). Ibrahim bin Adham removed the wine jar from the head and put it down there.

When the drunken man saw him there, he took the instrument from the singer and hit it on Ibrahim bin Adham's head with such force that the head started bleeding, and the instrument was also broken.

Ibrahim bin Adham left the place and came to river Dajla to remove blood from his head and clothes. Ascetics are different from other people. They also think differently.

Now, Ibrahim bin Adham did not worry about his head. He was worried that the young man's hand could be hurt when he was hitting, and the poor singer's instrument was also broken.

He tried to compensate them. He came home and could not find anything to give them. He took his prayer mat and sold it in Bazaar. He first went to the young man's home and gave half of the money he received by selling the prayer mat to the young man.

Ibrahim bin Adham said to the young man, "When you hit my head with the instrument, your hand was likely to hurt. It is the bestowment for that. Please accept it."

When the young man saw the excellent manner of Ibrahim bin Adham, he fell to his feet and asked for forgiveness. He repented from the core of his heart.

Ibrahim bin Adham then went to the singer's home and gave him the remaining half of the amount. He said, "Your musical instrument was broken due to my head. This money is a gift from my side to compensate for your loss. Please accept it."

When the singer saw such unmatched politeness of Ibrahim bin Adham, he also fell on his feet and repented.

Lesson: No matter how strong and powerful you are against your opponent, always make sure that you remain humble and behave justly. Dignity is not to demonstrate power and humiliate others, but it is in by showing humbleness.

Politeness and good manners can show miracles. It can help achieve things that cannot be achieved through force and anger. Politeness makes people lovable.

A Responsible Leader

One night Hazrat Umar (RA) was going on his usual round in a suburb of Madinah with his slave, Aslam, when they saw a distant fire in the desert. He said, "There seems to be a camp. It may be a caravan that was unable to enter the town due to nightfall. Let's go and see if they need any help." When Hazrat Umar (RA) reached there, he found a woman with children. The woman had a pan of water over the fire while the children were crying.

Hazrat Umar (RA) greeted her with Salaam and, with her permission, went near her.

Hazrat Umar asked her, "Why are these children crying?"

The woman replied, "Because they are hungry."

Hazrat Umar inquired, "What is in the pan?"

The woman answered, "Only water to soothe the children, so they may go to sleep believing that food is being prepared for them. Ah! On the Day of Judgement, Allah will judge between Umar and me for neglecting me in my distress."

Umar (RA) said, "May Allah have mercy on you! How can Umar know of your distress?"

The woman responded, unaware that she was talking to Umar (RA), "While he is our Amir, he must keep himself informed about us."

Hazrat Umar (RA) returned to the town and went to the public treasury (Baitul-Mal) to fill a sack with flour, dates, fat and clothes and draw some money. When the sack was ready, he said to his slave, "Now put this sack on my back, Aslam."

Aslam requested, "No, please, Amir-ul-Momineen[14]! I shall carry this sack."

Umar refused to listen to Aslam, even on his persistent requests to allow him to carry the sack. Hazrat Umar (RA) remarked, "Will you carry my load on the Day of Judgement? I must carry this bag, for it is I who would be questioned (in the Hereafter) about this woman."

Aslam most reluctantly placed the bag on Umar's (RA) back, who carried it right to the woman's tent with a swift pace. Aslam followed him on the way toward the woman. The children were crying when they reached there. He put a little flour and some dates and fat in the pan and began to stir. He blew (with his mouth) into the fire to kindle it.

Aslam says, "I saw the smoke passing through his thick beard."

After some time, the food was ready. He himself served it to the family. When they had finished the meal, he made over to them the little that was left for their next meal.

After their meal, the children were very happy and began to play about merrily.

The woman felt very grateful and said, "May Allah reward you for your kindness! In fact, you deserve to take the place of Khalifah instead of Umar."

Umar consoled her and replied, "When you come to see the Khalifah, you will find me there."

He sat for a while at a place close by and watched the children, and then returned to Madinah. On his way back, he said to Aslam, "Do you know why I sat there, Aslam? Because I had seen them weeping in distress; I liked to see them laughing and happy for some time."

*****

Prophet Muhammad's (PBUH) Companions were always afraid of the Day of Judgement. Hazrat Umar (RA) would often hold a straw in his hand and say, "I wish I were a straw like this." Sometimes he would say, "I wish my mother had not given birth to me."

Hazrat Abu Bakr (RA) is the most exalted person after the Prophet (PBUH). With all the virtues and privileges, he used to say, "I wish I were a tree that would be cut and done away with." Once, he went to a garden, where he saw a bird singing. He sighed deeply and said, "O, bird! How lucky you are! You eat, drink, and fly under the shade of the trees, and you fear no reckoning of the Day of Judgement. I wish I were just like you."

Lesson: Everyone would be accountable for their action on the Day of Judgement and would be asked about their actions and responsibilities. For instance, parents would be asked whether they looked after their children properly, and children would be asked whether they respected their parents. The day of Reckoning would be the final day where some people would be given eternal abiding in paradise, while for others, it would be a day of the greatest failure.

Hazrat Umar (RA) once said, "If a caller from Heaven announces that all people would enter paradise except for one person, I would fear that I will be that person. And if a caller had announced that all people would enter the Hellfire except one man, I hope that I will be that one person." It teaches us that we should spend our lives between fear and hope.

The Friend of Allah

The Prophet Ibrahim[15] (AS) was given the title of Khalilullah, which means "Friend of Allah".

The Noble Quran[16] says, "Who can be better in religion than one who submits his whole self to Allah, does good, and follows the way of Abraham the true in Faith? For Allah did take Abraham for a friend."

Ibn Abi Hatim writes that Hazrat Ibrahim (AS) had a habit of eating with guests. One day he was looking for a guest so that he could share his food with him, though he could not find anyone. When he returned home, he saw a stranger standing in his home.

He asked the person, "Who are you, and entered my home with whose permission?"

The stranger replied, "I entered the home at the order of the real owner of this house."

Prophet Ibrahim (AS) asked, "Who are you?"

The stranger said, "I am the Angel of Death and sent by God to convey the glad tidings to a person whom God made him his friend."

When Prophet Ibrahim (AS) heard that, he said, "You must tell me who that lucky pious person is. I swear by God that I will search for him no matter which part of the world he lives in. I shall meet him and spend all my life serving him."

When the Angel heard this, he said, "You are that person whom God has chosen."

He inquired, "Is it true?"

The angel replied, "Indeed, that is you."

Prophet Ibrahim (AS) asked, "Can you tell me what I have done that God made me His friend?"

The angel answered, "Because you give to everyone, but do not ask for yourself."

It is also narrated that, after receiving the Khalilullah's (Friend of Allah) title, the fear of God in his heart increased so much that his heartbeat sounded like a flying bird.

Lesson: Allah loves generous and selfless people. A guest is a blessing from God, and Allah likes those who look after their guests with respect and honour.

The Benefits of a Nobel Company

The story of 'the Companions of the Cave' (Ashab-e-Kahf) or 'the story of the Seven Sleepers' is an inspiring story mentioned in Surah Al Kahf in the Holy Quran.

The Companions of the Cave were people in the past who took refuge inside a cave from the tyranny of the cruel king, probably Decius (Duqyanus). The king was persecuting believers for their faith in one God. He ordered people to worship the idols.

One day a disciple of Jesus Christ visited that city and preached about the Oneness of God. He was acquainted with some youngsters of the elite class. The boys were accustomed to comfort and luxurious lives but still believed that the people were wrong to worshipping idols. Unlike their elders, they accepted the truth and rejected the false gods. So Allah increased their faith and guided them.

When the king noticed those youngsters' beliefs, he became furious. The king called them to the court and ordered them to abandon their new religion and return to their forefathers' religion of idolatry. The king threatened them by killing them for disobeying the order. They refused to succumb to him, rather inviting the king to the path of Allah.

The king decided not to kill them immediately and gave the boys time to think over, given the boys' immature minds and young age.

Meanwhile, the king went on a journey. The youngsters took it as an opportunity to run away from the town to protect their faith.

On their way, one of the men said, "I know a cave in the mountain. My father used to keep the sheep in it. Let us go there for a shelter."

They all agreed. On their way, a dog also followed them. These young people became worried when the dog started following them as the people might hear the dog barking and know of their whereabouts. They started throwing stones at the dog, but the dog was very persistent and was not giving up on them.

At last, the young men allowed the dog to come with them. They believed that God would protect all of them from harm. They continued walking until they reached the cave. They took some fruits and water. As the journey exhausted them, they lay down to take some rest.

Once, they all were asleep. God prolonged their sleep that day after day, year after year passed. Allah put them into a slumber in the cave, where they remained in a miraculous sleep for 300 years.

After sleeping for centuries, when Allah woke them up, they even could not feel any hunger. They asked one another about the length of the stay.

One person said, "We stayed here probably for one day or less than a day."

The other said, "It was morning when we went to sleep and look, now the sun is nearing to set."

Another said, "Let us stop discussing how long we remained asleep. Let's get some food. We should send one with money to buy some food. He should be careful not to alert anyone to ensure no one follows him to the cave; otherwise, the king guards would come after us here."

When one of the Companions was sent in search of food, he was surprised to see the remarkable changes in the city. Everything was different, but he could not comprehend why everything seemed to him unfamiliar.

He did not know for how long he and his friends slept. During that time, the cruel king died, and many others followed him and passed away. Now a pious king was ruling instead.

Being nervous and hesitant, he went to a shop to buy some food. When he took out his money and gave it to the shopkeeper, the seller wondered because the money had the picture of a king who had died centuries before. The shopkeeper thought that the stranger probably had found an old treasure. People gathered around him and eventually took him to their king.

When the king heard the story, he believed him as he had heard the story of the missing youngsters from his father and grandfather.

Along with the city's people, the king walked with the Companion of the Cave.

When they reached the cave, he said, "I will go inside first so that my friends do not get scared."

He went inside and informed his friends of what had happened. He told them that king Decius had passed away and that the present king was a pious Muslim. They were happy with the news.

When the group of these people died, their graves were made in that cave, along with the grave of the dog.

Moral: Keeping a good company can help not only in this world but can also lead to a better destination in the life to come. Even the dog achieved fame and was mentioned in the Noble Quran by staying with good people.

The general Divine rule of nature is that only human beings and jinns will be admitted into Heaven to be rewarded for their good deeds. However, some animals will be allowed to enter Paradise due to their virtues of companionship, which include the dog of Ashab-e-Kahaf, too.

Competition in Good Deeds

Hazrat Umar (RA) narrates that once, the Prophet (PBUH) asked for contributions in the path of Allah. In those days, I owned some wealth. I thought to myself, "Time and again, Abu Bakr (RA) has surpassed me in spending for the sake of Allah. By the Grace of Allah, I shall surpass him this time because I now have some wealth to spend."

I rushed home with the idea. I divided my whole property into two equal parts. One I left for my family, and the other, I presented to the Prophet (PBUH), who said to me, "Did you leave anything for your family, Umar?"

Umar (RA) replied, "Yes, O Prophet of Allah."

The Prophet (PBUH) said, "How much?"

Umar (RA) replied, "Exactly one-half."

By and by, Hazrat Abu Bakr (RA) came along with his donation for the cause. It transpired that he had brought everything that he possessed.

The Prophet (PBUH) asked, "What did you leave for your family, Abu Bakr?"

Hazrat Abu Bakr (RA) replied, "I have left Allah and His Prophet (PBUH) for them!"

Hazrat Umar (RA) says that on that day, he admitted to himself that he could never hope to surpass Hazrat Abu Bakr (RA) in doing good deeds.

This incident happened during the Battle of Tabuk when the Companions (Sahaba[17]) contributed beyond their means in response to the Prophet's (PBUH) appeal for help.

Lesson: This is an excellent example of a healthy emulation in sacrifice and is therefore quite desirable and welcome. People compete in worldly things such as having a better car, a beautiful house, etc. Similarly, they should compete in good works by donating more than others or praying more than their friends do.

Mahmud and Ayaz

Sultan Mahmud Ghaznavi and Ayaz are well-known personalities famous in history for their deeds and unprecedented relationship. Mahmud was a great warrior and conqueror who destroyed Somnath Temple's idol. On the contrary, Khwaja Ahmad Ayaz was a thin and ordinary-looking poor slave, but he was very close to Mahmud. Mahmud loved Ayaz because of his devotion and loyalty. Most aides were unhappy with the Sultan's affection towards Ayaz.

One day, a courtier commented that what is so special about Ayaz is that Sultan loves him so much. When the comment reached Mahmud, he became angry but decided to answer these jealous people at the right time. Coincidently, soon on one occasion, when the Sultan was on a journey, one of the camels fully loaded with precious stuff slipped. A chest of pearls broke, and the precious stones were spread out on the ground.

Sultan announced, "Everyone is free to pick anything they want." Everyone rushed to collect things for themselves, except Ayaz.

Sultan asked Ayaz, "Did you collect anything for yourself?"

He courteously answered, "No. Why would I even collect things as I am here to serve you? Why I would leave your service and collect things?"

After hearing this, Sultan addressed those who were jealous of Ayaz and said that this selfless love of Ayaz for me caused my love and affection for him.

*****

On another occasion, the Sultan and Ayaz were taking their lunch. The Sultan cut a slice of a cucumber and passed it to Ayaz, who ate it with relish.

After a while, he gave another slice of cucumber to Ayaz and took one himself.

But when Mahmud took a bit of the cucumber, he spat it out, as it was distasteful and bitter.

He accused Ayaz of tricking him into eating the distasteful vegetable by pretending it was delicious.

Ayaz answered, "No, my Sultan. It was delicious, as I received so many wonderful things from your hand that whatever comes from you is sweet to me."

*****

There are several similar stories of Ayaz's dedication to Sultan Mahmud. One day, ministers came to Sultan Mahmud and alleged Ayaz of stealing ornaments and treasure. They told Sultan that he kept them in a locked room, and he had been seen visiting it daily.

Upon hearing this, Sultan Mahmud Ghaznavi did not believe what the detractors told him. But to end their doubt and prove the great status of Ayaz, he ordered to search the place.

However, when the officials searched the room, they could not find any precious things except a worn cotton sheet and a pair of old slippers. No one there believed that Ayaz would visit his room every day just for a torn sheet and old slippers.

They thought the treasure must be buried underground and started digging the room floor, though they found nothing.

Eventually, the envious ministers informed the ruler about their failure and asked for forgiveness from the Sultan. Ayaz was summoned and asked why he kept the old torn stuff in a locked room and why he visited the room every day.

Ayaz replied, "Before I was your slave, I had worn that particular garb. But after joining your service, I was blessed with everything. I frequently visit the room to see my old dress so that I may remind myself who I really was so I do not fall into vanity."

After hearing this, the Sultan was highly impressed with his dedication.

Moral: Ayaz rose from the position of an enslaved person to the rank of an officer and then general in the army of Sultan Mahmud. His rise to power was a reward for his devotion to his master. The love between the two became an exemplary Islamic legend.

When people remind themselves who they are and their life's purpose, they will not go astray. In front of Allah, we are all His slaves, and we should not forget all the blessings and favours He has bestowed upon us.

The Devoted Student

The Madrasa (Islamic school), in which Imam Ghazali (Rah) was studying, was built by King Nizamul Mulk Thosi. Once, someone informed the king, "Oh, king! All the graduates from your madrasa are worldly-minded and materialistic. They are not taking any religious jobs that could help spread Islam."

The king said, "Well, the main purpose of the Madrasa is to make Islamic scholars who would support our religion. If these students are studying there to seek a job for money, then what is the point of spending so much money on them? They can then go to any other school."

He was thinking of closing the Madrasa, but he then thought to visit the madrasa and see the situation personally.

He planned a visit to the Madrasa while being incognito so that no one could recognise him, and through that way, he could learn the reality of what was happening there.

When he reached there, no one recognised him. He looked just like an ordinary person wandering around. He asked questions from students about why they were at the Madrasa.

One student said, "My father is a jurist (Mufti), so I also want to be a jurist. Once I get that job, then all people will respect me."

The other replied, "My father is a judge (Qazi). So when I get graduated, then I would also be a judge."

The third told him, "The king respects religious scholars. I will become a religious scholar and will become the king's courtier. That will make me an influential person as I would be sitting near the king."

When the king heard all this, he thought that it was true that all the religious students in the Madrasa were only seeking worldly titles. He thought that what was the point of wasting his money on them?

When he was going out the door, he saw a student reading under the lamplight. The king thought, let's ask him as well. The under-covered king got near him and said, Salaam.

The student answered Walikum Assalm, and then started his study again.

The king asked the boy, "Why do you not talk to me?"

The student replied, "I am not here for talking."

The king asked, "So what has brought you here?"

He replied, "I came here to learn how to please my God and guide people. I am reading these books to learn knowledge and then act upon it."

That boy was Imam Ghazali, a great Islamic scholar. When the king heard this, he decided to keep the madrasa open just because of Imam Ghazali's good intention and the real purpose of the knowledge.

Lesson: One should get an education with a positive intention and aim to please Allah. Learning for the sake of sorting out some worldly affairs and getting a better job is a secondary objective of education.

Love for Learning

Hazrat Moulana Abdul Qadir Raipuri (Rah) was a great saint in India. He studied Hadith in Delhi under the auspices of Moulana Abdul Ali (Rah), the student of Hazrat Moulana Qasim Nanautavi (Rah). Whilst in Delhi, he also studied under Allama Anwar Shah Kashmiri (Rah) for a short period.

Moulana Raipuri experienced hardships during his student life but endured these with great patience. During his education, his admission was declined because there was no one to provide him with food. There was no cook in the madrasa, and local people had assumed responsibility for providing meals for students. The administrators were matching students with sponsored families. When Moulana Raipuri was told that there was not enough food, he proposed that he would take care of his own food. He was given admission on the condition that he would have to arrange for his food himself.

Moulana Raipuri used to study the whole day, and then at night time, he would go to the Bazaar and scavenge around the rubbish to collect peels and skins of fruits. He would clean them and eat them throughout the day. Out of extreme poverty, he used to eat the leaves of the trees, as he could not afford to have any food to eat.

During the severe winters in Delhi, he did not even possess a blanket to cover himself. He would roll himself up inside the mat (Mosque chatai), exposing his head and feet. This continued for an entire year until Allah eventually sent someone to the Musjid who provided him with a thick comfortable duvet.

Once, someone discarded an old blanket in the dump. He picked it up, washed it, and used it for 15 years. He would sit on it, sleep with it, cover himself with it in the cold, and perform prayers on it.

Moulana Raipuri never replied to any of his letters throughout his student days. Instead, he used to place all of his posts in a broken earthenware jar. After finishing his study at the end of the year, he would empty the jar and begin reading all of his correspondence. There always used to be a mix of the news; someone might have died, been sick, born, or got married, etc. He said, "If I had read these letters before, it would have distracted me from my studies." So, when he reached his village, he would go for condolences or congratulation to his relatives. They would also be happy that he remembered them the whole year.

*****

There are dozens of such stories where religious scholars used to only focus on their education. Shah Waliullah (Rah) was a prominent Muslim scholar. One day, his son Shah Abdul Aziz Dehlavi (Rah) asked for water during his studies. He sent a boy for water. When his father heard that Abdul Aziz's focus was on water rather than on his study, he was very upset. His wife told him not to be disappointed so quickly. Let him come, and we will find out.

She put some vinegar in the water and gave it to the boy for Shah Abdul Aziz. When Shah Abdul Aziz came home, his mother asked him, "My son, did you drink the water?" He replied with "Yes".

The mother asked, "How was the taste?" He replied, "I do not know. It was fine."

The mother then told his father. "Abdul Aziz was so thirsty that he did not realise the sourness of vinegar in his mouth. That means that it was a necessity and not disrespect and lack of attention towards his study."

When Shah Waliullah heard this, he felt satisfied and prayed to Allah to maintain the love for knowledge in his family forever.

Lesson: Focus and respect for knowledge are very important. In the past, Islamic scholars endured so much in attaining knowledge. Despite extreme poverty, they continued their study. They did not complain about hunger or lack of food. Their focus was mainly on attaining education. Due to such dedication, people still remember their name after hundreds of years.

Respect for Teachers

Anwar Shah Kashmiri (Rah) was a Kashmiri Muslim scholar and jurist who served as the fourth principal of the Darul Uloom Deoband (a renowned Islamic university in India). He was a student of Mahmud Hasan Deobandi (Rah) and participated in the Indian freedom struggle through the Jamiat Ulama-e-Hind.

Despite all these engagements, he was always found by his students in front of a book. He would never touch a book without ablutions (Wudhu) and would always sit respectfully in front of religious books. Allama Kashmiri had high respect for knowledge and books. If a book had notes on its sides, he would move himself to read the side notes rather than moving the book.

During the Silk Letter Movement (Tehreek-e-Reshmi Rumal), his teacher decided to migrate to Saudi Arabia. At that time, Allama Anwar Shah Kashmiri was a prominent scholar as well and teaching at the same Islamic University.

As Allama Kashmiri was once the student of Mahmud Hasan, Allam Khasmiri came to him and sat at his feet and asked, " O, my dear teacher! Whenever we need help, we always come to you for help. If you leave us now, what would we do without you?" Allama started crying and was sobbing like a child.

Mahmud Hasan gave him comfort and said, "Anwar Shah! When I was here, then you were consulting me. When I leave the place, people will come to you for learning knowledge."

After getting some solace, Anwar Shah Kashmiri returned to his students. At that time, Mahmud Hasan thought, "My student is so much caring about me and look at me, I am migrating to another country and taking so big step in my life, and I even do not have a teacher left so I could ask for prayer."

Then he thought about one of his teachers, Hazrat Qasim Nanthowi (Rah). He went to his home, knocked on the door, and called, "O Respected mother, this is Mahmud Hasan. If you have Hazrat Nanthowi's shoes, then please give me?"

Then, Mahmud Hasan put his teacher's shoes on his head and prayed, "O Allah! Today my teacher is not here, but I kept his shoes on my head. Oh, Allah, due to its affinity, takes me in your protection and succeeds me in my mission."

Lesson: Muslim scholars had great respect for their teachers. Allah favoured them with matchless knowledge and unparalleled understanding of their tremendous reverence for teachers.

Allah gives teachers the second-highest status after parents because people learn knowledge through them. There is a saying that the teacher is not a king himself, but he makes kings.

Clothes and the Real Status

Sheikh Saadi Shirazi (Rah) was a prominent Persian poet and prose writer of the medieval period. His two books, Bustan and Gulistan, are still very famous. In one of his stories, he said that there was a discussion on a matter at a judge's (Qazi) office one day.

During the discussion, a man who seemed like a mendicant (Darvish) in poor dress entered the court and sat with others. The people in the room considered him an ordinary poor man and moved him to a place near shoes. The Darvish became very upset but uttered nothing.

The discussion was on a critical scholarly matter. No one could come up with the right solution. Soon the discussion heated up and was getting out of control. Everyone was trying to reject each other's arguments.

Darvish was sitting quietly and hearing the whole useless discussion. At last, he stood up and loudly addressed the participants. He said, "If you allow me, can I say something about the issue you are all fighting on?" The magistrate quickly permitted him, as he was desperately looking for a solution.

Darvish politely and nicely explained the solution for the matter with proper arguments. It surprised all the people in the meeting to hear about the straightforward solution to their complex matter.

People then realised that the person wrapped in the worn dress was a great scholar who easily resolved their issue. Qazi quickly stood up, removed his turban, and presented to that poor fellow. He said that we are sorry that we were unaware of your knowledge. In fact, you are the rightful person for this turban.

Darvish refused to take the turban and left the place by saying, "I do not want this arrogance-full bundle upon my head."

Remember that a person's status does not rise with better clothing but with better knowledge. A person cannot become a scholar due to his big head; otherwise, a pumpkin has the largest head in all."

Lesson: A morally poor person is worse than a financially poor person. We should not look at who is speaking and what their status is. But we should listen to what that person has to say.

The Memory of Imam Bukhari

Muhammad ibn Ismail Al-Bukhari (Rah), commonly known as Imam Bukhari, was a Persian Islamic scholar born in Bukhara (early Khorasan and currently Uzbekistan). He compiled the collected Hadith in a book known as Sahih Al-Bukhari, which Muslims regard as the most authentic (Sahih) Hadith collection.

One day he travelled to a place. At that time, he was quite young but very famous due to his knowledge of Hadith. Ten Muhaditheen (interpreters of Hadith) in that city decided to test Imam Bukhari's knowledge of Hadith. Each one prepared ten different Hadith in such a way that they mixed up the wordings and sources. In total, they all were supposed to ask one hundred Hadith.

A large number of people gathered to see the test. Though Imam Bukhari was very young, people knew about his memory power and Hadith skills.

When the test started, the first scholar stood and asked his first Hadith.

Imam Bukhari said, "I do not know."

All the people were surprised to hear the answer.

The Muhaddith (interpreter of Hadith) then asked his other nine Hadith, and Imam Bukhari answered, "I do not know" to all of them.

The congregation was shocked to see that he did not answer any Hadith.

Similarly, the other nine Muhadditheen also took turns and asked ten Hadith. But Imam Bukhari kept saying, "I do not know".

When the ten scholars finished their turns, Imam Bukhari started talking and told them, "Listen to me now. I will tell you about your Hadith now".

He then recited all the hundred Hadith in the same sequence as the ten Muhadditheen asked. He provided all the sources and the correct wordings. Above all, he repeated the exact wrong wordings that Muhadditheen intentionally made to test his knowledge. Imam Bukhari pointed out where they made the errors and with corrections.

Lesson: Hadith are the most authentic reference for Muslims after Quran. Today, if we know these Hadith, that is because of the hard work and efforts of scholars like Imam Bukhari.

They took the responsibility to travel by foot from one city to another to collect Hadith. Allah helped them by giving them such a memory that everyone admired.

An Obedient Son

Owais Qarni (RA) was a Muslim from Yemen who lived during the lifetime of the Prophet Muhammad (PBUH). Although he lived during the lifetime of Prophet Muhammad (PBUH), he never physically met him, so he is not counted among the Companions of the Prophet.

When he was very young, his father died. Owais (RA) accepted Islam and developed a profound love for Islam and the Messenger (PBUH). Owais (RA) and the Prophet (PBUH) never met because he stayed in Yemen taking care of his mother. Owais (RA) learned that there is an excellent reward in Islam for serving parents. His mother was sick and blind. So he devoted himself solely to the service of his mother.

One day, his mother permitted him to visit Madina to meet Muhammad (PBUH). However, she asked him to come back as soon as possible, as there was no one behind to look after her. In Madina, he discovered that Muhammad (PBUH) was out of the city. Owais (RA) did not stay there and returned home without meeting Muhammad (PBUH).

When the Prophet returned home, he was told that someone had come to see him, but he was in a hurry and returned. When Muhammad (PBUH) heard this, he was glad to hear that he had visited him. The Holy Prophet (PBUH) knew about Qarni (RA) and his love for him. He once told Hazrat

Umar Ibn Khattab (RA) about Qarni (RA) and had predicted that Hazrat Umar would meet Qarni (RA) after his (the Prophet's) departure from the world. He gave all the details about Owais and advised him to seek prayers for forgiveness and Ummah.

Other Companions asked if they could see him, but the Holy Prophet (PBUH) replied: "No, only Umar bin Khattab (RA) and Ali (RA) would meet him," and gave identity marks of Qarni (RA).

He directed Hazrat Umar and Hazrat Ali, "When you see him, convey my Salaam and ask him to pray for my Ummah."

Then the Prophet (PBUH) said, "He has served his mother so well that whenever he raises his hands to ask Allah, Allah doesn't send those hands back empty."

During Prophet's (PBUH) last days, he asked Umar (RA) and Ali (RA) to pass his Jubba (the blessed cloak) to Qarni (RA) and ask him to pray for forgiveness of the Muslim Ummah. This demonstrates the exalted status of Qarni (RA).

One day, Hazrat Umar and Hazrat Ali (RA) went to Kofa to meet Qarni (RA). They found him in a deserted place, praying under a tree whilst the camels were grazing around him. They then sat down and waited for Owais to finish his prayers.

When he finished, Hazrat Umar (RA) asked, "Who are you?" He replied, "I am a worker." He asked, "What is your name?" He replied, "Abdullah (The servant of Allah)" Umar (RA) then said, "We are all the servants of Allah. I am asking you the name which your mother called you with."

Owais Qarni (RA) did not recognise that they were Khalifah Umar (RA) and Ali (RA), as this was the first time of their meeting. After a long conversation, Owais Qarni (RA) was shocked and made Salaam to them, saying, "I apologise; I didn't recognise you."

Hazrat Umar (RA) said, "Raise your hands (in supplication for us), Raise your hands."

He exclaimed, "How can I raise my hands for you? Me? What is my significance that I make Dua for you?"

Umar (RA) replied, "Yes, we were ordered by the Prophet (PBUH); if you see Owais, then you must ask for his Dua. When he raises his hands for Dua, it is answered." Then Owais Qarni (RA) made a Dua for them.

*****

There are uncountable stories of the reward of obeying parents. Hazrat Bayazid Bastami, a great saint of his time, said he was awarded sainthood due to respect for his mother. Someone asked him how.

He said, "One night, my mother woke up and asked me for a glass of water. I rushed to bring her some water. I searched around the house, and there was no water. I went outside to the spring to get some water. When I came back, my mother was asleep. So, I stayed beside her bed with the glass of water. It was almost dawn when she woke up. She was surprised to find me around her bed. I told her the story. Then, she took the water, drank it, and prayed for me. At that moment, I felt a change in my life."

*****

Hazrat Abul Hasan Al-Kharaqani was a great saint. He had a brother who was busy worshipping day and night. One night, his brother was busy in the worship of Allah that he heard a Divine call in which it was told that "We have granted Our mercy on your brother and for his sake, We have also granted mercy upon you."

When he heard this call, he was surprised to hear that, in fact, he was worshipping Allah, so what was the reason that Allah forgave his brother and not him, and for his brother's sake, Allah granted mercy on him.

And he heard again a Divine call in which he was told, "We do not want your worship, and we will prefer and like the sincerity of the person who is in service of his mother."

Lesson: Owais Qarni (RA) gained this status by serving his mother and his love for the Prophet Muhammad (PBUH). This was to tell people how to serve their mothers and show the status of mothers in Islam. Even Umar (RA) and Ali (RA) asked Qarni (RA) to raise his hands to pray for them.

Disobedience to Mothers

Once, when the Holy Prophet (PBUH) was talking to his Companions (RA), a man came and addressed him, "O, Messenger of Allah! A young man is breathing his last. He is asked to recite Kalima, but he cannot do so."

The Holy Prophet (PBUH) asked, "Was he not reciting the Kalima at his lifetime?" The man said, "Yes, he was reciting it."

The Holy Prophet (PBUH) said, "If a person recites Kalima throughout his lifetime, then there is no reason why the person would not be able to say so."

Then the Prophet (PBUH) accompanied the man and other Companions (RA) present at that time to the house of the dying young man. The man was at the end of his life journey. The Messenger of Allah advised him to recite Kalima.

The man replied that he could not do so as the words would not come out of his mouth.

The Holy Prophet (PBUH) asked, "What is the reason?"

The young man replied, "It could be because I was disobedient to my mother."

The Holy Prophet (PBUH) then asked, "Is your mother alive?"

He said, "Yes."

The Holy Prophet (PBUH) called for the dying man's mother, whom he had disobeyed persistently.

When his aged mother came, the Holy Prophet (PBUH) asked, "Is he your son?"

She replied, "Yes".

He then asked her, "If we threaten to throw your son in a raging fire, will you recommend him to be forgiven?"

The lady replied, "She would definitely do so at that time."

The Holy Prophet (PBUH) then said to her, "If so, declare, making Allah and me your witnesses, that you are now pleased with him."

The old woman readily declared, "O Allah, you and your Messenger be my witnesses that I am pleased with this beloved son of mine."

Just after that, the Holy Prophet (PBUH) turned to the dying man and asked him to recite "Kalima".

By virtue of his mother's forgiveness, he found the words flowing out of his mouth, and he recited the Kalima "la ilaha illallah muhammadur rasulullah (There is no god but God, and Muhammad is the Messenger of God)."

Seeing this, the Holy Prophet (PBUH) praised Almighty Allah, saying, "Thanks to Almighty Allah that He saved this man from the fearful fire of Hell through me."

Lesson: Prophet Muhammad (PBUH) cursed the person whose old parents were alive, and he still did not earn Heaven (by serving them). So we must respect our parents. The happiness of God is in the happiness of parents.

Once a person came to the Holy Prophet (PBUH) and asked, "O Holy Messenger of Allah, who is the most deserving person to get nice treatment from me?" He replied, "Your mother." He asked, "Who is next?" To this, he got the same reply. When he repeated this question for the fourth time, he was told by the Holy Prophet, "Your father."

A Boy and Robbers

Abdul Qadir Jilani (Rah) was a great Muslim preacher, ascetic, and mystic. He had a great love for knowledge since his childhood. When he was eighteen, he took permission from his mother to travel to Baghdad for further education. At that time, Baghdad was the centre of learning in the world. During the journey, an incident happened that changed the lives of so many people.

When he was going out on his journey, his mother gave him forty gold coins. She sewed the coins into the lining of his coat for safekeeping. She advised her son always to speak the truth, no matter how terrible could be the circumstances. He promised that he would always speak the truth.

On his journey to Baghdad, robbers attacked the caravan. The thugs started searching the travellers and taking all of their valuables.

One robber came to Abdul Qadir and searched him, but could not find any valuables.

While searching, the robber asked Abdul Qadir, "Do you have anything valuable?"

Abdul Qadir calmly replied, "Yes, I have forty gold coins."

On hearing this, the robber started laughing and did not believe him.

Meanwhile, another robber came and searched him but could not find anything. He also asked him whether he had anything precious.

Abdul Qadir repeated the same answer and mentioned the forty gold coins. The robber also did not take him seriously due to his clothes and conditions.

Somehow, the leader of the robbers, Ahmed Badawi, heard this and asked to bring the boy to him.

The leader asked Abdul Qadir, "Are you hiding any valuables?"

Again Abdul Qadir said, "I already told your companions about the forty gold coins."

The leader then asked, "Where are they?"

He said, "They are hidden and sewed under the cover of his coat."

When they opened up the seams of his clothes, they found exactly forty gold coins.

Now Abdul Qadir's declaration of the valuables perplexed the robbers. The leader said, "We never knew that you had so much money. You knew that we were bandits and looting travellers. Why did you tell us about the forty gold coins? You could easily hide them from us."

Abdul Qadir said, "My mother advised me always to tell the truth. My mother's advice is more precious to me than the gold coins."

The bandit chief was overcome with remorse and told his companions, "This young boy did not break his mother's promise and had an unshakeable faith in God. Shame on me that I have been disloyal to my promise with Allah."

Holding his head down in shame, tears started rolling down his face. He cried bitterly and then fell to the feet of Abdul Qadir and repented for his sins.

When his accomplices saw this, they too did likewise and repented sincerely from all their sins. The leader of the robbers told his henchmen to return everything to the travellers.

Lesson: Honesty and truthfulness is the foundation for a fair and just society. Besides a lesson on truthfulness, there is also another lesson, which is listening to parents. All parents want their children to be successful and have a better life. Therefore, we should listen to their advice.

Hazrat Huzaifa in the Battle of the Ditch

The Battle of the Trench (Battle of Khandaq) was a 27-day-long defence by the Muslims of Medina. Muslims endured severe hardships as 10,000 enemies surrounded them.

It was a freezing night. Muhammad (PBUH) came to his Companions (RA) and told them that Angel Jibraeel came down and said that the Almighty Allah has heard your appeal, accepted your supplication and ordered the wind along with the angels to drive away the enemy and their army. So the wind uprooted the tents of idolaters, and all of them prepared to run away from there.

Hazrat Muhammad (PBUH) then asked who would enter the enemy camp and bring me information about them. I promise a paradise as a reward for such a person. No one volunteered as they were in terrible condition due to starvation and cold.

Muhammad (PBUH) then went back and prayed and came out and said, "The person who goes to the enemy camp, I give him comfort that he would come back safely and be my companion in paradise." No one volunteered again as hunger, cold, and fear overcame them.

At last, Muhammad (PBUH) called for Huzaifa (RA), who was sleeping. The Holy Prophet called him again and received no reply. On the third time, Huzaifa (RA) replied, "Here I am, O Messenger of Allah."

The Holy Prophet (PBUH) said, "I am calling you, but you don't reply."

He said: "May my parents be sacrificed on you. I could not speak due to the severity of cold and hunger."

The Holy Prophet (PBUH) said: "Go and find out the circumstances of Quraish and don't do anything before returning to me."

Hazrat Huzaifa (RA) stood up, shivering and trembling, scared and cold. The Prophet (PBUH) made a prayer for him, "O Allah, protect him from in front of him and from behind, and from his right and from his left, and from on top and from below."

By the miracle of the Holy Prophet's supplication, God removed his fear and all cold. He became so warm as if he was in a heated bath. When he entered the army of Quraish, he saw a huge tent, and he walked towards it.

Hazrat Huzaifa (RA) says, "I saw that they had prepared a fire which went off and on. When I looked carefully, it was Abu Sufyan's tent (the leader of Quraish). He was sitting near the fire and shivering from the cold. And he said he had a clear shot of Abu Sufyan and was about to take his arrow and shoot him, but then he remembered the commandment of the Prophet (PBUH) to be discrete, 'Hide yourself and us from them' so he stopped, sat down, and continued finding out what's happening."

Shortly afterwards, Abu Sufyan stood and addressed his men, "O people of the Quraish, I am about to make a statement to you which I fear would reach Muhammad (PBUH). Therefore, let every man among you look and make sure who is sitting next to him."

On hearing this, Huzaifa (RA) immediately grasped the hand of the man next to him and asked, "Who are you?" (Putting him on the defensive and clearing himself).

Abu Sufyan went on, "O people of the Quraish, you are not in a safe and secure place. Our horses and camels have perished. The Banu Qurayza has deserted us, and we have had unpleasant news about them. This cold wind buffers us. Our fires do not light, and our uprooted tents offer no protection. So get moving. For myself, I am leaving." He went to his camel, untethered it, and mounted on it. He struck it, and it stood upright.

Hazrat Huzaifa (RA) said, "I had another clear shot of Abu Sufyan, but I remembered what the Prophet (PBUH) said, so I let him go."

Huzaifa (RA) said that if Muhammad (PBUH) had not instructed him not to do anything until I returned to him, I would have killed Abu Sufyan then and there with an arrow.

With this news, Huzaifa (RA) returned to the Prophet (PBUH). When Huzaifa returned to the camp, he found the

Prophet (PBUH) praying, so he waited. Prophet Muhammad (PBUH) was wearing the shawl of one of his wives, so when he saw his state, he gestured for him to come into the shawl. Huzaifa (RA) slept till morning until the Prophet (PBUH) came and woke him up.

Lesson: There are several lessons in this story. Obeying the Prophet is an important lesson there. Even Huzaifa (RA) could kill the enemies' leader at once, but he did not, as he had been instructed just to spy and do nothing else.

Another lesson is that whenever the Prophet (PBUH) faced trouble, he would take comfort in prayers.

The other takeaway from this story is that Allah's help comes in different forms. On that occasion, it was a storm that destroyed the enemy camps. So, following Allah and the Prophet Muhammad's (PBUH) commandments, Allah provides help that could be beyond human imagination.

The Test of Leper, Bald and Blind

Abu Huraira narrated that he heard Muhammad (PBUH) saying that Allah willed to test three Israelites: a leper, a blind man and a bald man. The story goes like this:

Allah sent them an angel who came to the leper and said, "What would you like the most?" He replied, "Good complexion and good skin, and riddance of that for which people have considered me unclean."

The angel passed his hand over him, and his illness was cured, and he was given a good complexion. Then the angel asked, "What kind of property do you like best?"

He replied, "Camels."

So the leper was given a pregnant she-camel in her tenth-month pregnancy. The angel prayed, "May Allah bless you for this."

Then the angel went to the bald man and said, "What thing do you like the most?"

He said, "Good hair and wish to be cured of this disease, for which people dislike me."

The angel touched him, and his baldness disappeared as he acquired a full head of hair.

The angel asked, "And what would you like to have?"

He replied, "Cattle."

The angel gave him a pregnant cow and said, "God bless you for this."

Then the angel came to the blind man and asked, "What thing would you like the most?"

He said, "That God may restore my vision so I can see people."

The angel passed his hand over him, and Allah restored his eyesight.

The angel asked him, "And what would you like to have?"

He replied, "Sheep."

The angel gave him a pregnant ewe and said, "God bless you for this."

Afterwards, all the three pregnant animals gave birth to young ones and multiplied and brought forth so much that eventually, one of the men had a valley full of camels, the other had a valley full of cattle, and the third one had a valley full of sheep.

Then the angel came to the leper in disguise and said, "I am a poor man who has lost all means of livelihood while on a journey. So none will satisfy my need except Allah and then you. In the name of Him Who has given you such nice complexion and beautiful skin, and so much wealth, I ask you to give me a camel so that I may reach my destination."

The man replied, "I have many obligations (so I cannot give you)."

The angel said, "I seem to know you. Were you not a leper to whom the people had a strong aversion? Weren't you a poor man, and Allah gave you (all this property)?"

He replied, "I simply inherited this wealth, grown generation after generation."

The angel said, "If you are telling a lie, let Allah make you as before."

Then the angel came to the formerly bald man in disguise and spoke to him as he had to the former leper. And the formerly bald man replied, as had the leper. So the angel said, "If you are telling a lie, let Allah make you as you were before."

Then the angel finally came to the formerly blind man and said, "I am a poor man and a traveller, whose means of livelihood have been exhausted while on a journey. I have nobody to help me except Allah, and after Him, yourself. I ask you by the One who restored your vision for a sheep to help me over on my way."

The man said, "I used to be blind, but God restored my eyesight. Take whatever you want, and leave what you will. By God, I will give you no trouble about anything you take today for the sake of God."

The angel said, "Keep what you have. You have been tested, and Allah is pleased with you and is angry with the other two."

Lesson: Allah gives wealth to people and can test them to see if they appreciate His blessing. Sometimes people get miser, and they do not want to spend their money. They indulge in their wealth so much that they earn money just to have more of it. Their whole purpose of life is to accumulate more money. Allah does not like such people. He likes those who spend on the needy and poor people.

A Terrified Slave

One day, Bahlool (a saint) was on a ship with some other passengers. On the ship, there was a merchant who was accompanied by his slave. It was the first time that the salve was travelling on a ship. When the ship started sailing, he got scared of the ship's turbulent movements.

The slave started crying, "Take me out of the ship. The waves will destroy the ship. For God's sake, return the ship to the shore."

All the travellers became annoyed at the slave's behaviour. Some people were trying to comfort him and cool him down. But his panic was on the rise.

Bahlool came near the slave's master and asked, "If you give me permission, I can help remove your slave's fear." The merchant was already embarrassed and annoyed by his slave's behaviour, so he permitted him.

Bahlool gave the order to give the slave a few dips in the sea. The passengers started laughing and were surprised by Bahlool's suggestion. He said, "Do what I am saying, as his master has already given me permission." When the slave heard about the proposal, his crying became more violent.

Eventually, some people came forward and held the slave and plunged him into the water. The slave was fully immersed in the water and then removed for breathing. He was shouting, "Save me! Save me!" But the people did not listen and gave him a few more dips.

When the slave was brought to the board, he took out water from his nose and mouth. After that experience, he quietly sat in the corner of the ship and did not make a sound. He stopped all the crying at once, which he was doing before the drowning experience.

The travellers asked Bahlool the reason why this act calmed the slave down.

Bahlool replied with a smile, "It is simple. He did not know how comfortable the ship was or how great and valuable it was until he was thrown away into the sea. After finding the harsh reality of water, he then understood the value of the ship that how comfortable and relieving place it was."

Lesson: We sometimes do not understand how many blessings we have from God. We always complain about what we do not have, making our lives miserable. The urge to have more takes us on those paths where greed covers our eyes. If we compare ourselves to those who do not have such facilities that we enjoy, we may realise how comfortable our lives are.

A Slave with a Dog

Once Abdullah Bin Jafar (RA) passed by an orchard in Medina, of which the caretaker was an Abyssinian slave.

Abdullah Bin Jafar (RA) saw the slave taking food while a dog was sitting in front of him. Every time the slave put a morsel of food into his mouth, he threw another morsel, as big as his own, onto the dog. Ibn Jafar (RA) stood watching for a while. When the meal was finished, he went over to the slave and asked him, "Who is your master?"

The slave replied that he belonged to the descendants of Hazrat Uthman[18] (RA).

Ibne Jafar said, "I saw you were doing something very strange."

The slave asked him what it was, and Jafar (RA) said, "After each morsel of food you took, you gave another to your dog."

The slave replied, "This dog has been my companion for many years, and I must give it a fair share of my food."

Ibne Jafar (RA) said, "A dog can be fed on something of inferior quality."

The slave said, "I feel ashamed to face Allah that I should eat while one of His creatures is watching me with a hungry look."

After this, Abdullah Bin Jafar (RA) came back, went to the descendants of Uthman and said that he had come to ask for a favour. When they said, "Please let us know," he replied that he wanted to buy such a garden. They told him, "We will be happy to present you the garden as a gift."

They insisted on accepting it free of charge, but he said that he must buy it on payment. At last, the price was fixed, and Ibne Jafar (RA) purchased the garden. He then said he also wanted to have the slave working in the garden.

They requested that they should be excused, as the slave had been with them since his childhood, and they would be grieved to part from him. But when Ibne Jafar (R) insisted, they agreed to let him have the slave.

After purchasing the garden and the slave, Ibne Jafar (RA) went to the garden and said to the slave, "I have bought this garden and yourself." The slave congratulated him on the bargain and said, "May Allah bless you in the deal; only I am grieved at parting from my masters who have brought me up since my childhood."

Abdullah bin Jafar (RA) said, "I set you free, and let this garden be my parting gift to you."

"Hearing this, the slave said, "If so, I call you to witness that I make this garden a private Wakf (endowment) for the descendants of Uthman (RA)."

Abdullah bin Jafar (RA) says, "I was greatly surprised to hear this from him, and I went home, invoking Allah's blessings upon him."

*****

Once, a person presented a gift of five hundred dirhams to Sheikh Junaid Baghdadi (a great saint) and requested that the amount be distributed among the Sheikh's students and disciples.

The Sheikh said to him, "Do you possess any more dirhams?"

The man said that he had a lot of them in his possession.

The Sheikh asked him, "Do you wish to increase your wealth, or are you content with what you possess?"

The man replied that he desired an increase in his wealth.

The Sheikh responded, "Then, your need is greater than ours as we do not wish for an increase in what we possess in the world."

Sheikh Junaid Baghdadi (Rah) then declined to accept the gift and gave the money back.

Lesson: Such were the excellent qualities and proud achievements of the slaves of our Muslim ancestors! Even today, a rich person wants more money, and the poor would not miss any opportunity to become rich.

Great Altruism

Hazrat Abu-Jahm-bin-Huzaifah (RA) narrates:

During the battle of Yarmuk, I searched for my cousin, who was at the forefront of the fight. I also took some water with me for him. I found him in the very thick of battle in the last throes of death. I advanced to help him with the little water that I had.

Soon, however, another sorely wounded soldier beside him groaned, and my cousin averted his face and beckoned me to take the water to that person first.

I went to this other person with the water. He turned out to be Hishaam bin Abil Aas (RA). Hardly had I reached him when the groan of yet another person lying not very far off was heard. Hisham (RA), too, waved me in his direction.

Alas, before I could approach him, he took his last breath. I made all haste back to Hishaam (RA) and found him dead as well. Then, I hurried as fast as I could to my cousin, and, lo! In the meantime, he had also joined the other two.

Lesson: There are many similar incidents of such self-denial and heroic sacrifices in the books of Hadith. This is the extreme demonstration of self-sacrifice, where each dying person was foregoing, slaking his thirst in favour of his other needy friend.

We should look around and try to help others forsake some of our own pleasures for others, such as sharing food and donating money.

Musa (AS) with a Beggar and a Shepherd

Once Musa[19] (AS) was on his way to Mount Sinai, where he came across a beggar. The beggar asked him, "I am very poor and do not have anything. Ask God to give me something and make my life prosperous."

Musa (AS) replied that he would ask Allah for you.

As he further travelled, a shepherd came to him and asked him, "He is prosperous and cannot control his wealth now. The cattle and other assets are increasing day by day." He asked Musa (AS) to pray to God for the reduction in his wealth. Musa (AS) also promised him that he would ask Allah about his situation.

When Musa (AS) returned from Mount Sinai, he saw the shepherd who asked him about the prayer.

Musa (AS) told the shepherd that I got the answer, "Allah said to tell the shepherd to be unthankful to me."

The shepherd replied, "O Musa, how I can be ungrateful to God? He gives me so much. I must be thankful to God for bestowing on me all the wealth."

Musa (AS) replied, "Then your wealth will not diminish, but will keep growing."

Shepherd said, "I do not care then, but I must obey and be thankful to my beloved God."

As Musa (AS) went further, he saw the beggar who asked him about his question.

Musa (AS) told the beggar that God says, "Tell the beggar to thank Me. I always give to those who are grateful to Me."

The beggar replied, "O Musa! How can I be thankful to God? What does he give me? I am a poor person. I would not be thankful to Him unless he makes me prosperous."

Musa (AS) then said, "In that case, you will remain destitute, and your situation would not be better off."

Lesson: The main takeaway from this story is that we should be thankful to Allah in every situation. We should be thankful to God, no matter how difficult the situation could be.

If someone is poor, he still should be thankful to Allah that he has eyes, tongue, ears, and good health. We should always look down and compare ourselves with those who are in a worse situation than ours. Then, we would become grateful to Allah.

Prophet Yousaf (AS) and a Boy

Once there was famine, and Hazrat Yousaf (AS) was the governor at that time. People were coming to him and getting rations for their survival. As the food was scarce, everyone was getting a small limited amount of staples. Among the people, a boy came to collect the food and then talked to Hazrat Yousaf (AS). After hearing something from the boy, Yousaf (AS) became so happy that he gave him more food and gifts.

Allah knew what happened between the two, but he still sent revelation to Yusaf (AS), "Oh, Prophet, why did you give him so much?"

Hazrat Yousaf (AS) replied, "Oh God, he told me that he was that few months old baby in the cradle who miraculously testified my innocence when Zulaykha falsely accused me. When I heard this from him, I was delighted. As he once gave evidence of my innocence, I thought, now he is in need, so why not help him."

God revealed at that time on Hazrat Yousaf (AS), "O Yousaf, a person who once gives a testimony that you are chaste, you give him immensely. When a person testifies my greatness and comes to me on the Day of Judgement, I will give him according to my glory."

Lesson: When we do Zikir (remembering Allah) or reciting the Quran, that is all testifying Allah's greatness and our acceptance that Allah is Great and we are His slaves. When Allah hears that his human being is testifying His greatness, He would be pleased with us in this world and the Hereafter.

A Needle Worth of Sin

Once there was a great scholar. When he died, one of his students saw him in a dream. He saw that the teacher was barefooted, without clothes, and wandering restlessly in a desert in a hot summer. He seemed so worried and tense.

The student asked him, "Oh, my dear teacher! You always led people to the right path and spread God's words. What happened to you today? Did Allah not accept your worship?"

He replied, "Allah accepted everything. But I am now facing this terrible situation due to a needle."

The student surprisingly asked, "How?"

The scholar explained, "I borrowed a needle to sew my clothes before death. But I left it in my cupboard and forgot to return it to my neighbour. And after that, I died. Now what you see is because of that needle. You must go to my house and tell my family to find the needle in my cupboard and return it to the owner."

When the student woke up in the morning, he went to his late teacher's home and told the whole story he saw in his dream.

The family looked for the needle and found it, which the teacher mentioned in the dream. The family confirmed that they knew about the borrowed needle from the neighbour. But they were busy with guests coming for condolence, so that is why its return was delayed.

The student asked for the needle so he could quickly return it to that neighbour and end his teacher's torture.

The student then rushed and returned the needle to its owner. He told the neighbour how much the teacher suffered due to the needle and requested forgiveness for his teacher. The neighbour cried that if such a small and trivial mistake caused such a terrible punishment, what would be the punishment for the major sins.

The next night, the student saw that his teacher was in a paradise and was surrounded by servants.

The student went near him, paid Salam to him and asked, "O, my dear teacher! How do you feel now?"

The teacher smiled and said, "When you returned that needle to the neighbour, and he forgave my mistake at that time, Allah ceased my punishment and bestowed all these blessings on me which you see around me now."

Moral: No matter how small or big a sin could be, we should ask forgiveness from the victim. Allah likes those who seek forgiveness from the victims.

No Virtue is Small

nce upon a time, there ruled over Bokhara, a ruthless ruler who, one day, was riding a horse when he saw a mangy dog shivering from cold. He was moved to tears and told one of his servants to take the dog to his house and care for it till his return from the ride. He went on his errand and came back in the evening.

On coming back home, he called for the dog, had it tethered in the corner of his house, served it with food and drink, and told his servants to massage the dog with oil and cover it with blankets to protect it against the cold.

Then he lit a fire to keep it warm and comfortable. Two days later, the ruler died. A saint was aware of the ruler's cruelty and wrong-doings. The saint saw him in a dream and asked him, "How did Allah deal with you?"

The ruler said, "When I was brought before Allah, He told me, 'You were (like) a dog (because you behaved in cruel, beastly, inhuman ways), but We have granted you forgiveness (because of your kind act) by showing mercy to a dog.' Then, in His infinite mercy, Allah took upon Himself the requital of all my cruelties and wrongs doings."

*****

In the dream, someone saw Imam Ghazali (Rah), a great scholar, and asked, "How did Allah Almighty deal with you?"

He replied, "Allah Almighty forgave me."

The person asked, "What was the reason for being forgiven? Which book earned you the blessing?"

He answered: "None of the books and good actions earned me but a fly which sat on my pen to drink ink, and so I stopped writing until it had done so and flew away. That was the deed. Allah liked it and forgave me."

Lesson: One should seek Allah's pleasure at all times. No virtue is insignificant as a man never knows which of his deeds might please Allah.

A Devil's Tree

Once there was a tree which somehow became very popular in the village. People started believing that the tree was very sacred, and anyone who prayed for the tree got their wishes answered. People started worshipping it. In that village, a very pious person was spending most of his time at home worshipping Allah.

Some villagers visited the pious person and told him about the tree. When he heard that, the people started worshipping a tree instead of Allah; he became furious, took his axe and was on his way to cutting the tree.

While he was on the way to cut the tree, Satan personified himself in the form of a human and asked him, "Where are you going?"

The pious man replied zealously, "I am on my way towards cutting that devil's tree, whom people have started worshipping."

Satan said, "Look, you are very near to Allah and should focus on your worship. You should not waste your time coming out home and cutting a tree. Let these ignorant villagers do whatever they do. Allah will help them if He wishes. But I think you should stay at home and pray for them and yourself."

The pious man replied, "I believe it is my duty to forbid people from worshipping anything else except Allah. No one can stop me from cutting it down."

Satan said, "I shall not allow you to cut that beautiful green tree. The people love it."

After a hot conversation, both started fighting. In seconds, the pious person grounded Satan, mounted on his chest, and started punching him. Satan soon realised that he could not beat the pious person. Satan then asked, "Wait and listen to me carefully, as I want to tell you something important."

The pious man paused to see what he was going to say now.

Satan said, "You are a pious person, not a Prophet. Did Allah give you any order to cut it down? Remember, it is not your duty to do such an act. It is fine if you think worshipping a tree is not good. You should avoid yourself worshipping that tree."

Satan kept talking and convincing him that cutting the tree was not a good idea, though the pious man stood on his decision and said, "No matter what, I will cut the tree down."

They both again grappled, and Satan was on the ground again. The pious person sat on his chest. But before he started punching again, Satan shouted, "Wait for a moment. I have a better solution now. But first, you get off my chest and let me get up."

Satan started explaining, "There is nothing in fighting with each other. I respect those who dedicate their lives to Allah. But I know you do not have enough food. If you had money, you would not even come out from home for work. But you have to feed your family, and sometimes you and your family starve. Even you do not have any savings. When you die, what would happen to your wife and poor children?"

Satan carried on, "Would you not like to have some money so you would fully dedicate yourself to worship Allah?"

The pious person thought for a while and said, "Yes, but how?"

Satan replied, "Then spare the tree. It would not make any difference. If you cut this tree, later on, people will turn to another one. For you, the important task is to go home, look after your family, and continue your worship. You do not have to go out to work every day. You will find a gold coin under your pillow every morning."

The pious man thought that the stranger (Satan) was right. What would I do if they kept growing such trees again and again? So he accepted the proposal and returned home without cutting the tree.

The next day when he woke up, he was pleased to see a gold coin under his cushion. He was collecting one gold coin under his pillow for the next few days. One day when he woke up, there was no gold coin. He searched here and there but found none. The pious man got angry and thought about cutting the tree to give a lesson to that dodgy stranger who broke his promise of the daily gold coin.

On his way, he again met the same stranger (Satan). The stranger asked him, "Where are you going?"

He replied, "I am going after cutting that tree."

"No, you must not. I will not allow you to do that," challenged the stranger.

Their argument leads to the fight again. But this time, Satan, with a single push, grounded the pious man, set on his chest, and threatened him, "If you do not give up the idea of cutting the tree, then I will kill you."

The pious man tried his best to fight back, but could not get out of Satan's grip. Losing the fight, the pious man asked Satan, "Tell me! A few days ago, I trounced you, but what happened today? Why am I so weak, and you are so strong?"

Satan laughed and said, "It is a matter of intention. The first time when we faced each other, your intention of cutting a tree was just exclusively for Allah. But today, your intention is partly for a gold coin and not solely for Allah. Your faith was not strong, so I defeated you."

Lesson: When a person acts with a good intention, Allah supports the person in that action. Prophet Muhammad (PBUH) said, "The deeds depend on the intention." Satan will never stop whispering bad intentions into our hearts, so we must remember Allah. If someone wants to become a doctor to help sick people and support poor people, Allah will also support the person in achieving the goal, and that person will get a reward from Allah in paradise accordingly. But if a person wants to become a doctor to get rich and only care about money is only beneficial in this world. He would become a doctor but would not get all those blessings as a person with good intentions.

Satan's Tricks

Wahb ibn Munabbih (Rah) narrates that there was a pious person in Bani Israel. Satan tried to deceive him, but in vain. The pious person one day went outside. Satan took this as an opportunity and tried to develop evil thoughts in his heart, but was again unsuccessful. He tried to scare him through a big rock bringing near his head. However, by the name of God, it went off. Then Satan came in the form of a lion and other scary animals. But the pious person did not give any attention to such threats and ignored him.

Satan turned itself into a snake and came toward him when he was praying. It wrapped itself from his foot and then crawled through his body and reached to his head. When the pious person went to prostrate, it spread all over his face. When he was prostrating, the snake opened its mouth like trying to take a bite of his face. But the pious person was removing it without being interrupted during his prayers.

Once he finished his prayers, Satan said, "I tried all my best to distract you, but I could not win from you. Now I want to make a friendship with you, and from now onwards, I will not try to mislead you."

The pious person replied, "Not at all. Due to the Grace of Allah, neither I am scared of you nor do I need your friendship."

Satan asked him, "Ask me about your family. What will happen to them when you die?"

The pious person replied, "By then, I would be dead. So that would not be a concern of mine."

Satan asked him, "Then ask me about how I misguide human beings."

The pious person said, "Yes, tell me how you misguide human beings."

Satan then said, "With three things, miserliness, anger and intoxication. When a person becomes a miser, I turn the wealth insufficient in front of him. Then he stopped spending as Allah commands and started keeping his eyes on other people's wealth.

"When a person gets angry, I play with that person as children play with a ball. I can make him commit anything, no matter how knowledgeable he could be. Anger makes him blind.

"When a person gets drunk, I can lead the person towards wicked acts like someone is taking a goat holding from the ear."

*****

There was an older man on Noah's Ark, and no one recognised him. Hazrat Noah (AS) brought a pair of everything to the Ark, but this old man was sitting alone.

People presented the old person in front of the Prophet Noah (AS).

Prophet Noah (AS) asked the old person, "Who are you?"

The old person replied, "I am Satan."

Noah said, "How dare you come on the Ark? You cannot stay here. You have to leave."

Satan asked, "Please forgive and allow me to be on the Ark."

Noah (AS) said, "We will spare you on one condition that you promise to tell us your deadliest tricks, which are the most harmful for human beings."

Satan said, "I can tell you those on one condition that you would allow me on the Ark."

After the Prophet (AS) agreed, Satan said, "I harm people the most through jealousy and greed. I was also the victim of jealousy, turning me from a holy angel to the devil. Whereas greed expelled Adam from paradise."

Lesson: People commit serious crimes when they are angry or drunk. Indeed, jealousy and greed are also two major spiritual diseases that lay the foundation for other moral issues. People usually fight either because of jealousy or due to their greed. The Prophet (PBUH) said, "Beware of envy, for it devours good deeds just as fire devours wood or grass." On another occasion, the Prophet Muhammad (PBUH) said, "Look at those who are lower (poor) than you, but do not look at those who are above (rich) you, lest you belittle the favours Allah conferred upon you."

Evil Thoughts

Hazrat Dr Abdul Hai was a Pakistani Muslim scholar and a Sufi mentor. One day a person came to him and asked, "I am perturbed about my prayers. It seems that my prayers are worthless. When I pray, so many worldly thoughts come to mind. When I prostrate in prayers, God forbid, so many wild thoughts fill my mind. What sort of prostrate that could be? I think it is useless. I do not know how to get rid of these evil thoughts."

Dr Hai said, "When you go to prostrate to Allah, what do you think, how are your prayers?"

He replied, "Horrible and disgusting because it is full of worldly and evil thoughts."

Dr Hai told him, "No one should do such a dirty and unpleasant prostration to Allah. Because Allah is Pure, there should be the best prostration for Him. Why not you do such an awful prostration to me?"

The person said, "Astaghfirullah (I seek forgiveness in God). Oh my God, why should I prostrate to you?"

Dr Hai said, "That means your prostration is just for Allah. Your head would not bow toward anyone else. No matter how dirty and bad thoughts cross your mind during the prayers. Your head will go down only for Allah and no one else. If these thoughts come unintentionally, then they would not do any harm to you. Allah would not make you accountable for those."

Lesson: Five times' prayers are compulsory. Every Muslim should make provision to perform them at their specified time. A person should ensure that no thoughts other than focusing on prayers come to mind while performing prayers. However, unintentional worldly thoughts may come sometimes, and InshAllah would not punish us for them. The thought process is like a road. On the road, people cross each other; they can be rich and poor; black and white; good and evil; young and old.

Similarly, all sorts of thoughts may come to mind. They can be good or bad. We should ensure that we make friends with good ones.

Conceit

There was once a young man who committed so many sins. He was on the river bank and was crying and wailing for forgiveness.

Nearby there was a pious and ascetic person who saw him. He became so enraged by looking at the sinful person. What is this accursed person doing here? He is the fuel of Hellfire, and maybe Hell will also take refuge from him.

He thought about him and prayed to God, "Oh God, please do not place us together in the life Hereafter."

When he finished his prayers, Allah revealed to Jesus Christ that the sinful person asked for forgiveness for his sins, so I accepted his repentance. In return, I announced paradise for him. I also accepted the prayers of the pious person. He asked not to be treated as the sinner, so his place is now Hell, as they both cannot be in the same place.

The pious person felt superiority owing to his worship and piousness over the sinful one; therefore, he wasted all his good deeds. Whereas the sinner was remorseful and sought forgiveness from Allah, he was rewarded paradise in return.

Lesson: No matter how good a person becomes, he should not feel arrogant and consider himself superior. Considering others as inferiors is a great sin. May Allah save us from being arrogant. Satan (Iblis) also once considered himself superior to Adam and disobeyed Allah's command to prostrate to Adam and thus became Satan.

Deceiving and Treachery

Sheikh Muhammad bin Ismail Bukhari did a huge favour to the Muslim Ummah by collecting the Hadith. His book, Sahih Bukhari, is the second-highest sacred book after the Holy Quran.

One day Imam Bukhari travelled to see a man to collect a Hadith for his book. When he reached there, the man was trying to get hold of his horse. The horse had run away from him and stood at a distance. The man then lifted his shirt and acted as if he had been holding pasture's grass inside it to bring the horse towards him. He was trying to tempt the horse towards him. Eventually, the horse started to come toward the person, and as soon as the horse came near, he caught it.

Imam Bukhari was watching all this. Imam then asked the man if he did have grass in his shirt, to which he replied, "No, I only did it to get hold of the horse."

The Imam exclaimed, "How can I take a blessed Hadith of the Holy Prophet (PBUH) from a man who lies to animals?" He left the man there without quoting Hadith from him.

Lesson: No matter how small the deception could be, it should be avoided. There is a saying that little drops of water make the mighty ocean. Prophet Muhammad (PBUH) says that a black mark appears upon a believer's heart when he sins. His heart will be polished if he abandons the sin, seeks forgiveness, and repents. If he returns to the sin, the blackness will be increased until it overcomes his heart.

Bad Intention

There is an old story that once a slave of a king ran away. The king sent his soldiers after him. They found him after a long search and took him back into their custody. The soldiers brought him to the king. The Wazir (a ranked high minister) disliked that slave. He thought it was a good opportunity to get rid of the slave.

He advised the king to kill the slave and make him a symbol for other enslaved people. So, others may not be able to do a similar act in the future.

When the slave heard that, he, with folded hands, humbly addressed the king, "You are my king, and I obey you. However, if you kill me, I am afraid that on the Day of Judgement, you will find yourself in big trouble for killing an innocent person."

"Because you are my lord, and I love you so much, I do not like to see you in such trouble. So, please allow me to kill your Wazir and then you can kill me in retribution. In this situation, my killing will be lawful for you, and you will not be held accountable for it on the Day of Judgement."

When the king heard this, he laughed and asked the Wazir, "What is your opinion about this proposal?"

When the Wazir realised that his plans did not work against the slave, he bowed before the king and said, "My lord, my opinion is to free this slave in the name of God for the blessing of your deceased elders. It is better to let him go before he puts me in another problem."

Lesson: It is important to understand that when you want to start enmity against someone, that means that you may also be on your enemy's target. It is better to avoid doing bad planning against others.

Anger Control

One day Imam Abu Hanifa went home to sleep after Zuhr prayer. His habit was to spend his night awake praying while taking a nap after Zuhr's prayers, after spending the whole day teaching. His room was upstairs, with many steps to climb to reach the entrance. No sooner had he climbed up the steps to lie down for some rest than somebody knocked on the door.

Imam Abu Hanifa could ignore the person and take his nap. Everyone in the town knew that it was his sleep time. Therefore, he should not have been disturbed at such a time. However, when he came down and opened the door, a person was standing at the door. Imam Abu Hanifa asked him how he could help. The person said, "I wish to ask you a question."

Imam Abu Hanifa politely asked, "What is the question you wish to ask?"

The person replied, "Oh! When I was coming, I remembered it. But now I forgot."

Imam Abu Hanifa said, "It is not a problem. When you remember, you can ask me."

Imam Abu Hanifa went back up the stairs. Just as he was about to lie down for sleep, someone again knocked on the door. Imam Abu Hanifa came down, and when he opened the door, he saw the same person again. The person said, "I had remembered the question, but just as you reached near the door, I forgot it."

Imam Abu Hanifa did not get upset or frustrated by this situation and told him to ask him the question after remembering it.

Imam Abu Hanifa climbed up again and lay down on the bed. There was again knocking on the door. He came down and found the same person standing at the door.

When he inquired again, "What is the question?"

The person replied, "Now I remember. I want to know what is the taste of faeces?" Imagine, if it was another person, he could burst out of anger.

But Imam Abu Hanifa responded very calmly, "It depends. The taste of fresh faeces is sweet, whereas the taste of stale faeces is bitter."

The person said, "How do you know? Have you tasted it?"

Imam Abu Hanifa replied, "There is no necessity for one to taste to determine these attributes. One can use common sense to find the answer. Flies are attracted by sweetness and tend to settle on freshly passed faeces. That implies that freshly passed faeces taste sweet. Flies do not set on stale faeces as bitterness repels flies, which implies that stale faeces are bitter."

The person then apologised for the inconvenience he had caused to Imam Abu Hanifa. The person then further said that we were a few friends having a discussion. I argued that Hazrat Sufyan al-Thawri is the most patient and even-minded person, while others argued that it was you. We selected the wrong time and awkward questions for the test to incite you. But today, you have proved that you may be the most good-tempered and equable person on the earth.

*****

On another occasion, Imam Abu Hanifa had been teaching his students when a person came and started swearing at him. Imam Abu Hanifa did not pay any attention to him, and neither stopped his teaching. He also told his students to avoid the person.

When Imam Abu Hanifa finished his lesson and began walking on his way home, that person started going with Imam Abu Hanifa and continued his verbal abuse.

When Imam Abu Hanifa reached his home, he stopped at his door and said, "This is my home. I have to go inside now." He then entered his home, but the person continued swearing at him. Imam Abu Hanifa did not retaliate.

The abuser then shouted, "Am I like a dog to you who is barking at you?"

A reply came from inside the house. "Yes."

Lesson: Anger is one of the worst things considered in Islam. Islam teaches love, and Muslims should avoid getting angry. The Great Imam exhibited that we should show patience at all times. When we try to find good in bad things, our anger may start to vanish. Sometimes anger may make people miserable, and later they regret it.

A King versus a Lame Mosquito

Nimrod is a biblical figure and was described as a king who ruled over ancient Mesopotamia (now known as the State of Iraq). Nimrod, the mighty hunter, was one of the sons of Kush. Whereas Kush was the son of Ham, the lowest and least important of Prophet Noah's three sons. Nimrod came from a line that Prophet Noah (AS) cursed.

By birth, Nimrod had no right to be the king or ruler. But he was a mighty strong, sly and tricky person, and a great hunter. His followers grew in number, and soon Nimrod became the mighty king of Babylon, and his empire extended over other great cities.

Nimrod was an intelligent king, but his intelligence was blinded by arrogance. He claimed to be a god and ordered his people to treat him like God. However, Prophet Ibrahim (AS) opposed him and invited him to believe in Allah.

Nimrod invited Prophet Ibrahim (AS) to his palace and asked him, "O Abraham, who is your Lord?"

Prophet Ibrahim (AS) replied, "My Lord is Allah Who gives life and death."

Nimrod ordered two of his prisoners from the jail and ordered one's head cut off and the other be left free. Then, he told Abraham (PBUH), "Have you seen how I gave life to one and death to other! The one with a death sentence, I set him free, while the other with just imprisonment, I cut off his head."

Thus, Nimrod showed such a shallow and cheap interpretation of life and death. He was then asked by Ibrahim (PBUH) if he could raise the sun from the west. At this time, he had no answer. He was clearly not the almighty being.

He hated Prophet Ibrahim (AS) more as he considered him his enemy and wanted to destroy him. Nimrod very rudely said, "If He is the God of Heaven, I am the god of the earth. Where are His armies? If the sky fell on my troops, they could hold it up with their lances. Tell Him I challenge Him to a battle. He has no say on the earth. The whole earth belongs to me."

A few days later, Nimrod gathered his army and marched it towards the place of Prophet Ibrahim (AS) and his people. When faced with the Prophet Ibrahim (AS), Nimrod challenged him arrogantly, "Tell your God and his army against my troops and me!"

And shortly after that, suddenly, a black cloud emerged in the sky. Both sides observed the black cloud. But the closer the black cloud got, the louder the sound became. The people then realised that it was not a black cloud but a flock of mosquitoes.

When the order was given, the host of mosquitoes hurled themselves against the army of the enemy of Allah. They filled the soldiers' mouths, eyes and ears while biting and wreaking vengeance on the army of Nimrod.

In a short time, destruction had overtaken Nimrod's army. Nimrod himself left the battlefield, taking refuge in one of his castles. He thought he had saved his life by closing down all doors and windows.

Despite the great miracle he had witnessed, Nimrod could not bring himself to repent and accept the Oneness of Allah. How could he do so without overcoming his arrogance and pride? The scoundrel was wilfully obstinate in his disbelief.

Allah had chosen one lame mosquito with a damaged wing for killing Nimrod. The lame mosquito made its way, limping to the castle where Nimrud was hiding. It went through a keyhole and settled on Nimrud's knee. Nimrud spotted the insect and tried to kill it, but the mosquito settled on his other knee. Nimrud still could not kill the mosquito despite making all his efforts, which then went up inside his nose.

The mosquito started chewing on his brain. The pain was so severe that it caused constant headaches. Nimrud appointed servants to hit him on the head with wooden mallets. The blows were giving him a brief respite by interrupting the mosquito's movements. As soon as the insect began eating his brain once more, he would cry, "Hit me! Hit me!"

The so-called "god of the earth" was being beaten by his servants. Even those coming to see him were asked to slap his head rather than greet him. One day, one of his servants wielded the mallet too hard, and Nimrud's evil head cracked, and he died.

Lesson: We should learn from this story that arrogance and pride lead to nothing but destruction in both worlds. Nimrud gave himself such a high status that he considered himself to be God, yet he was disgracefully defeated by one of Allah's weakest and most humble creatures.

We should remind ourselves of the Power of Allah and His Bounties to keep arrogance and pride at bay. We should understand that everything we achieve is due to Allah's blessings upon us, not because of our doings.

Shaddad's Paradise on Earth

One day, the Angel of Death said to God that I took the souls of countless people, but two deaths saddened me. One was an infant on a shipwreck when I took his mother's soul, and another was a person named, Shaddad. I obeyed your command and took their souls.

On one occasion, a ship was sunken, and a woman with her infant child survived. They both were on a wooden plank in the water. At your command, oh Allah, I took the woman's soul. I was worried about what would happen to the boy, as his mother was dead then. The infant was on the floating wood and could fall into the water at anytime. The little boy had no food, and there was no one to look after.

The laundry workers washing clothes at the riverbank saw the boy on the wooden plank. They were surprised to see that the mother was dead while the boy was alive. They took the boy to their chieftain. As he had no kids, he took him as his responsibility and adopted him as his son.

When Shaddad was nine years old, once he was playing with other kids one day. They heard that the king was passing by. Everyone ran to see the king, but he was standing there alone. The king was followed by his foot soldiers. One of his soldiers found a small sack of antimony. The soldier's eyesight was poor, and he was trying to test it on someone else to ensure it was safe.

He asked the boy to come, putting the antimony in his eyes. Soon the boy started seeing treasures down the earth. The boy was very sharp-minded, and he started crying and pretended pain due to antimony. The soldier then threw away the sack hopelessly, considering it was useless and harmful. The boy picked up the sack and ran to the father. He told the whole story.

The chieftain became overjoyed. He said we have people; you would use the antimony and guide us where to dig for the treasure. So they started a treasure hunt, and soon they became super-rich. When the boy reached his youth, he was aware of all the treasure. Soon, he became the tribe chief and then slowly challenged the king, and after defeating him, he became the king himself.

When he became king, he ordered to build a paradise city on earth, where the building bricks were made out of gold and silver. He ordered to build a marvels garden that should have all the luxury things. When the city was ready, he planned to visit it. When he reached the door of the city, the Angel of Death took his soul, and he had got no opportunity to see his paradise.

So the Angel of Death said to God, oh God, I was also very saddened taking his soul as his paradise city was ready, and he even had not seen it. Allah told the Angel of Death that the boy who survived the shipwreck was no one but Shaddad himself.

Despite surviving, he disobeyed my commandments, which is why he did not even get time to see his own built paradise. It is believed that Shaddad's paradise still exists, but Allah hid it from the people.

Moral: Shaddad should have been thankful to God that He bestows on him so much blessing, but instead, he chose the wrong path. That is why God did not allow him even to enter his paradise. We should always obey God's commandments so that God may be kind to us and make our lives peaceful in this world and Hereafter.

The Last Person Leaving the Hell

Once, people asked Prophet Muhammad (PBUH), "O Allah's Messenger! Shall we see our Lord on the Day of Resurrection?"

He replied, "Do you have any doubt in seeing the moon on a full-moon night when there are no clouds?"

They replied, "No, O Allah's Messenger!"

He said, "Do you have any doubt about seeing the sun when there are no clouds?"

They replied, "No, O Allah's Messenger."

He said, "You will see Allah (your Lord) in the same way. On the Day of Resurrection, people will be gathered, and He will order the people to follow what they used to worship. Some of them will follow the sun. Some people will follow the moon, and some will follow other (false) deities, and only this nation (Muslims) will be left with its hypocrites. Allah will come to them and say, 'I am your Lord.' They will say, 'We shall stay in this place till our Lord comes to us, and when our Lord comes, we will recognise Him.' Then Allah will come to them again and say, 'I am your Lord.' They will say, 'You are our Lord.'

"Allah will call them, and As-Sirat (a slippery bridge) on which there will be clamps and hooks like the thorn of

Sadan will be laid across the Hell, and I (Muhammad PBUH) shall be the first amongst the Messengers to cross it with my followers. Nobody, except the Messengers, will then be able to speak, and they will say, 'O Allah! Save us, O Allah! Save us.' There will be hooks, like the thorns of Sadan in Hell. Have you seen the thorns of Sadan?"

The people said, "Yes."

He said, "These hooks will be like the thorns of Sadan, but nobody except Allah knows their greatness in size, and these will entangle the people according to their deeds; some of them will fall and stay in Hell forever; others will receive punishment (torn into small pieces) and will get out of Hell till when Allah intends mercy on whomever, He likes amongst the people of Hell. He will order the angels to take those who worshipped none but Him Alone out of Hell. The angels will take them out by recognising them from the traces of prostrations, for Allah has forbidden the Fire (Hell) to eat away those traces. So they will come out of the Fire. The Fire will eat away from the whole human body except the marks of the prostrations. At that time, the inhabitants of Hell will come out of the Fire as mere skeletons. The Water of Life will be poured on them, and as a result, they will grow like the seeds growing on the bank of a flowing flood-water stream.

"Then when Allah finishes from the judgement amongst His creations, one man will be left between Hell and Paradise, and he will be the last person from the people of Hell to enter Paradise with his face towards Hell and say,

'O Allah! Turn my face from the Fire as its wind has dried me, and its steam has burned me.'"

"Allah will ask him, 'Will you ask for anything more in case this favour is granted to you?'"

"He will say, 'No, by Your (Honour) Power!'"

"And he will give his Lord (Allah) what he will of the pledges and the covenants. Allah will then turn his face from the Fire. When he faces Paradise and sees its charm, he will remain quiet as long as Allah wills."

"He then will say, 'O my Lord! Let me go to the gate of Paradise.'"

"Allah will ask him, 'Didn't you give pledges and make covenants (to the effect) that you would not ask for anything more than what you requested at first?'"

"He will say, 'O my Lord! Do not make me the most wretched amongst Your creatures.'"

"Allah will say, 'If this request is granted, will you then ask for anything else?'"

"He will say, 'No! By Your (Honour) Power! I shall not ask for anything else.'"

"Then, he will give his Lord what He wills of the pledges and the covenants. Allah will then let him go to the gate of Paradise. On reaching there and seeing its life, charm, and pleasures, he will remain quiet as long as Allah wills and then will say, 'O my Lord! Let me enter Paradise.'"

"Allah will say, 'May Allah be Merciful unto you, O son of Adam! How treacherous you are! Haven't you made covenants and given pledges that you will not ask for anything more than what you have been given?'"

"He will say, 'O my Lord! Do not make me the most wretched amongst Your creatures.' So, Allah will laugh and allow him to enter Paradise and will ask him to request as much as he likes. He will do so till all his desires have been fulfilled. Then Allah will say, 'Request more of such and such things.' Allah will remind him, and when all his desires and wishes have been fulfilled, Allah will say, 'All this is granted to you and a similar amount besides.'"

Lesson: Even those among the people, who may be destined for Hell, will eventually leave Hell, except the very worst - who refuse in this life - to repent to Allah. Truly, Allah is Most Merciful, All-Merciful and All-Forgiving!

The Repentance of Ibn Sabbath

Ibn Sabbath was a notorious thief in Baghdad city. He was so expert in his profession that the police never caught him. However, one night he was caught red-handed during a robbery. According to the law, the judge (Qazi) ordered for cutting his one arm and was sentenced to life imprisonment. The city took a sigh of relief. Since then, he had been known as a one-hand Satan.

After spending a few years in prison, he somehow escaped from prison. Losing one arm and spending a long time in prison had left no impact on him. He straight away started his old profession and planned a robbery. He was wandering around at night but could not get an opportunity. At last, he saw a big bungalow. He got near its gate and was planning to break into the bungalow. While contemplating, he found out that the door was left unlocked. He slowly opened the door and entered the courtyard.

Inside there were several rooms. He thought that the house could be owned by a big trader or a rich person. He saw one big room inside there, and he slowly moved towards it. Its door was also unlocked.

When he entered the room, he found it almost empty and could find nothing precious. He saw a mat made from date leaves, a leather cushion, cloth, and fabric rolls. When he looked at such trivial things around, he turned angry and started swearing at why the owner had accumulated such unworthy stuff in the room. He got very frustrated as he was expecting ornaments and pearls.

However, he did not want to leave the house empty-handed. So, he started gathering the cloth fabrics and made a pile out of them and tried to bind them with a cloth. However, he could not tie the knot.

Suddenly, someone entered the room with a lamp. Ibn Sabbath got scared. The person was tall, skinny, with a curvy back. He was wearing a light colour long gown and a black hat. Although the stranger was skinny, he was still comfortable and had mesmerising eyes.

After entering the room, he kept the lamp aside and addressed Ibn Sabbath, "God's mercy be on you, oh my brother, you cannot do this work alone and in the dark. I can assist you in your work."

Ibn Sabbath was shocked to hear this from the stranger. Before he could understand anything, the stranger started dividing clothes into two bundles and tied them up.

The stranger then addressed Ibn Sabbath, "Forgive me, my brother! I forget that you may be feeling starving after this hard work. Let me bring some hot milk. That would make you feel fresh."

The stranger went out of the room, and Ibn Sabbath was shocked by what was happening around him. Suddenly he realised how stupid he was for not understanding the stranger. Of course, he was also a thief like him. Ibn Sabbath was thinking about the stranger. He assumed that stranger was an insider who knew that no one would be at home. But now he saw me in the room. That is why he divided the cloth rolls into two bundles and would demand half of the share of the booty.

Meanwhile, the stranger came back with a cup full of milk and presented it to Ibn Sabbath. He told him to drink it to regain strength. Ibn Sabbath was feeling starving, so he drank all of it.

He then turned towards the stranger and said, "Look, I came first to the house, so based on the rule in our profession, you have no right on the swag. However, as you helped me, I would give a small portion of it."

The stranger smiled and told him, "Do not worry, as I would not take any share. However, I would help you and would not ask for any prize."

Ibn Sabbath ordered him, "I will take the small bundle as I have one hand, and you would take the heavy one and help me take it to my place."

Both agreed, and with that, Ibn Sabbath asked him to keep moving in front of him. The skinny person used all his power to lift the bundle, and his curvy back bent more. They started moving in a hurry.

However, Ibn Sabbath was in a hurry as the night was passing quickly. He kept scolding the stranger to get faster.

At one stage, the stranger fell down. Ibn Sabbath started swearing and kicking him.

The stranger apologised and stood up. He picked up the package and resumed their journey. Soon they reached an old building outside the city.

It was Ibn Sabbath's refuge place, and both of them unloaded the bundles there. Ibn Sabbath sighed relief and saw the stranger was out-breath, but his eyes were so mesmerising that he could not bear to look at him.

The stranger smiled and told him that he was the building owner, and all the things were his property, but now he gave him happily. He apologised for giving him trouble on the way and did not give him much hospitality. He took permission to leave and said goodbye.

The stranger quickly started walking towards the city. However, his words and actions substantially affected the thief.

Ibn Sabbath's whole life was spent in sins, and his heart was never touched by such an action before. He started thinking about whether it was a dream. He misbehaved with the stranger, and the stranger's behaviour in return was beyond praise.

He kept thinking about him and trying to digest the whole event. At last, he became so desperate that he went out for searching for the person. He was not afraid of anything; he just wanted to find the person and cry for forgiveness. He straightaway reached the house which he robbed at night time.

At the gate, he asked a wayfarer, "What is the merchant's name who owns this house?"

Surprisingly, the wayfarer looked at him and replied, "It seemed like you are a traveller and new in the city. This is not the house of any merchant. This house belongs to Sheikh Junaid Baghdadi (One of the greatest Muslim saints)."

Ibn Sabbath heard that name before but never saw his face. When he entered the house, he saw the opened door of the big room he had robbed at night. He saw the person whom he met last night. He was sitting on a mat, and dozens of people were sitting in front of him. Ibn Sabbath stayed at the door.

Meanwhile, there was Adhan (Islamic call to prayers) in a mosque, and everyone stood, and the room got empty. The Sheikh also then stood, and when he stepped outside the room, Ibn Sabbath fell to his feet and started crying. He wholeheartedly repented, and his dark heart started cleaning.

The Sheikh took him in his hands with love and patience and embraced him. Ibn Sabbath then became a different person.

For forty years, the world failed to change him, but Sheikh's patience and good morality changed him in a few moments. He joined the Sheikh, and from Ibn Sabbath, he became Sheikh Ahmad Ibn Sabbath (Rah).

Moral: Good manners, such as generosity, clemency, compassion, patience, contentment, love for obedience and pious deeds, are very powerful and can change people's lives.

The Repentance of Two Fire Worshipers

There was two fire worshipping brothers in Hazrat Malik Bin Dinar's (Rah) time. One day, the youngest brother told the eldest one, "You worshipped the fire for 73 years, and I worshipped it for 35 years. Let's test whether the fire would burn us like non-fire worshipers. If the fire burns us, we will stop worshipping it, and if it does not, we will continue our worship." They both agreed.

The elder one asked the younger to try first. When the younger brother put his hand on fire, it burned his finger, and he quickly removed his hand. He said, "Oh fire, I worshipped you all my life, and you burned my finger." The fire did the same thing as it did to the elder one.

The younger brother told the elder, why not repent and worship the real God? Both brothers agreed and searched for the right path. They decided to become Muslims.

They both went to Busra, and Hazrat Malik Bin Dinar was delivering a sermon. When the older brother saw him, he said, "I do not want to become Muslim. I spent all my life worshipping fire, and I do not want to give up on my ancestors' religion. Otherwise, our family will rebuke us. I will prefer Fire rather than revilement at the hands of my family."

The younger brother tried to explain to him that the insult faced by the family is nothing compared to the eternal punishment in the Hereafter. However, that unfortunate person could not understand and returned to his dark life.

The younger brother came to Hazrat Malik Bin Dinar with his wife and children. After the sermon, he told his story and asked him to make them Muslims. Therefore, Hazrat Malik Bin Dinar converted all of them to Islam.

When the newly converted Muslim was leaving, Malik Bin Dinar asked to wait so he could collect some donations for him from his students. The young man told him he did not need anything else.

He, with his family, started living in a house in a deserted place. The next day, his wife asked him to go out and search for a job so the family could survive. He went out and searched for a job, but all in vain. He could not find any job. He thought, why not work for God? He went far from people and started praying until evening. He returned home empty-handed and told his wife that he had started working for the king and would be paid tomorrow. The whole family went to sleep without any food.

He went again to Bazaar the next day but could not find any job there. He then spent his day worshipping God again. Upon returning home, he again told his wife that the king promised to pay the wages by Friday.

At last, the Friday also came, but no one hired him for a job. He again got busy in worship and spent the whole day in prayers. In his supplication, he thanked God for showing him the right path, and in the end, he begged God to find a way for economic means so he could focus more on worshipping him.

When he went for Friday's prayers in a mosque, his family was starving at home. At that time, someone knocked on the door. His wife saw a charming young boy holding a tray covered with golden cloth. The boy told her, "This is two days' wages of your husband and tell him that if he had done more work, then he could get more."

When the woman uncovered the tray, there were one thousand gold coins. The woman took one gold coin to a Christian goldsmith for sale. When the goldsmith weights the coin, it was over two mithqals. When the goldsmith saw the engraving on the coin, they seemed about the Hereafter. The goldsmith asked how she got the coin, and she told him the story. The goldsmith also became Muslim and gave her two thousand dirhams. He told her. "Spend these, and when it finishes, then inform me." After taking the money, she bought some food for cooking.

Unaware of the situation, the husband performed two rakaths' (units) prayer with great fear and humility after the evening prayer. He tied some sand in a cloth, thinking that when his wife asked for food, he would tell her that there was flour in it. When he reached home, he smelled food. He left the sandbag at the door so the wife would not know about it. When he entered home and asked about the food, the wife told the whole story. He went into prostration and thanked Allah's mercy upon his family.

Then the wife asked what was in the clothes which you left at the door? He said, "Do not ask me about it." He took the cloth so that he could throw the mud out of it. But to his surprise, he found flour instead of mud. He was shocked to see what had just happened. The turn of the event deeply touched him, and after that, he spent his whole life in worship till his death.

Moral: Belief in God from the core of the heart is fundamental. And that is the real faith. When we believe that Allah can do anything, then miracles start happening.

The Repentance of Habib Ajami

Habib Ibn Muhammad Al-Ajami Al-Basri (Rah) was a Muslim Sufi mystic, saint, and traditionalist of Persian descent. He settled in Basra, Iraq, where his shrine is. Before his reformation, he was a wealthy money-lender and offered loans on interest to the people. His daily routine was to visit his debtors and extract payment. He would not return without squeezing out a payment from his hard-pressed debtors. If debtors could not pay, he would levy a shoe leather charge for his wasted time. In this manner, he covered his daily expenditure.

One day, he had gone to look for a certain debtor. The man was not at home, and the debtor's wife told him that they had no money to repay the instalment. But Habib kicked the door and entered the house, saying that he must collect something today, no matter what.

"My husband is not at home. I have nothing to give you. We had slaughtered a sheep yesterday, but only the neck is left. If you like, I will give you that," the debtor's wife told him.

"That is something," the usurer replied, thinking that he might at least take the sheep's neck off her and carry it home.

Habib asked his wife, "Put a pot on the fire. And cook the meat."

"I have neither firewood nor flour for baking bread," the wife answered.

"Very well," he said. "I will go and fetch them as interest from debtors." So he went off and fetched these things, and the wife set the pot. When the food was ready, the woman was about to pour its contents into a bowl when a beggar knocked on the door. Habib rebuffed him, saying that there was nothing to give.

"If we give you what we have got," Habib shouted at him, you will not become rich, and we will become poor ourselves." The wife was trying to help the beggar, but in front of Habib, she was helpless. The beggar left crestfallen.

When Habib's wife opened the pot to dish out the food, she was shocked to discover its contents had turned into blood.

She was scared and hurried back, and taking Habib by the hand, she led him towards the pot and exclaimed, "Look what has happened to us because of your cursed usury and your shouting at the beggar! What will become of us now in this world, not to mention the next?"

The sight of the blood shocked Habib Ajami. His heart opened up, and he said to his wife, "Be witness that I repent and shall abstain from all evil deeds. I write off all the loans to my debtors."

The next day, he went out to look for his clients to waive all the monies owing to him. On his way, he saw children were playing in the street. When they sighted Habib, they shouted. "Here comes Habib, the usurer. Be careful! Do not let the dust under his feet contaminate you. We all will then become miserable like him." These words hurt Habib very much.

He then went to Hazrat Hasan Basri (Rah) and told the whole story. Basri (RA) counselling reduced him to tears. He repented and resolved to lead a life of piety.

As he returned from the meeting, he spotted one of his debtors, who made to run away. "Do not run away," Habib called him. "Till now, it was for you to flee from me; now I must run away from you."

As he proceeded home, he came across the same group of boys he had met earlier. They spoke among themselves, "Give way! Habib is returning after having repented. Let not our dirt fall on him least Allah records us as transgressors."

In sheer elation, Habib Ajmi exclaimed, "O Allah! Only today have I repented, and You have so quickly exalted my name."

Habib then issued a proclamation. "Whoever wants anything from Habib, come and take it!" The people gathered together, and he gave away all his possessions so that he was left penniless. Another man came with a demand. Having nothing left, Habib gave him his wife's shawl. To another claimant, he gave his own shirt.

He went to a hermitage on the banks of the Euphrates (a famous river) and dedicated himself to the worship of God.

Every night and day, he studied under Hasan Basri, but he could not learn the Quran, for which reason he was nicknamed the Barbarian (Al-Ajami). Time passed, and he was completely destitute. His wife asked him for housekeeping money constantly. So Habib left his house and made for the hermitage to resume his devotions.

When night came, he returned to his wife. His wife demanded, "Where have you been working, not to bring anything home?"

Habib replied, "The One I have been working for is extremely Generous. He is so Generous that I am ashamed to ask Him for anything. When the proper time comes, He will pay me. The master says, 'Every ten days, I pay the wages.'"

So Habib repaired daily to the hermitage to worship till ten days were up. On the tenth day, at the time of the midday prayer, a thought entered his mind. "What can I take home tonight, and what am I to tell my wife?" And he pondered this deeply.

Meanwhile, Almighty God sent a porter to the door of his house with a sack of flour, a skinned sheep, oil, honey and three hundred dirhams. The handsome young porter told Habib's wife that these came from the master and told Habib, "You do more, and we will increase your wages."

At nightfall, Habib proceeded homeward, ashamed and sorrowful. As he approached his house, the aroma of bread and cooking assailed his nostrils. His wife ran to greet him and cried, "The man you are working for is very generous".

She told the entire story. Habib was amazed and exclaimed, "I worked for ten days, and he did me all this kindness. If I work harder, who knows what he will do?" And he turned his face away from worldly things and gave himself up to God's service.

Lesson: Allah tests humans to a certain extent to see which person has true faith in Him. One lesson from the story is that when Habib learned that Allah did not like his action, he did not find excuses but promised to change his life. Allah then gave him a more honourable life in this life and raised his status in the life to come.

The Repentance of a Killer

In the Prophet Musa (AS) times, a man from Bani Israel had mercilessly murdered ninety-nine people. Then, he felt remorse. He went to a monk and told him about his past, explaining that he wished to repent and become a better person.

He asked, "I wonder if Allah accepts my repentance?"

The monk replied negatively and told him that his sins were too much to be forgiven, and he had to go to Hell, as God would not pardon his evil actions.

When the killer heard that, he got angry and blasted, "Then I may kill you, too." He then killed him and completed one hundred.

He (the murderer) then found out about another scholar. He reached him and said that he had killed one hundred people and asked him if there was any chance for his repentance to be accepted.

Being a truly wise man, the scholar replied in the affirmative and replied, "Who stands between you and repentance? Of course, you will be pardoned."

The scholar then asked him, "Go to such and such land; there (you will find) people devoted to worship of Allah.

Join them in worship, and do not return to your land because it is an evil place."

The man expressed repentance and regret. So he went away and hardly had he covered half the distance when death overtook him. There was a dispute between the angels of mercy and the angels of punishment as they came to take away his soul.

The angels of mercy pleaded, "This man has come with a repenting heart to Allah," The angels of punishment argued, "He never did a virtuous deed in his life."

Then another angel appeared in the form of a human being, and the contending angels agreed to make him an arbiter between them.

He said, "Measure the distance between the two lands. He will be considered belonging to the land to which he is nearer." They measured the ground and found him closer to the land (of piety) where he intended to go.

Because the man had just set out, he was far from his destination. But because he was sincere in his repentance, the Lord moved the spot where he was laid and brought near the good people's city. Thus, angels of mercy collected his soul.

The above story was based on a Hadith from Sahih Bukhari Volume 4, Book 56, Number 676.

Lesson: The wicked person did not do one single kind act. But since he embarked upon the journey to Allah, Allah did not reject him and accepted his repentance. No matter how much a person could be sinful, Allah would forgive if the person repented with sincerity.

Another lesson in the story is that when looking for counselling and advice, ask advice from the best one. The killer first asked a person who was not very learned, but eventually, he found the right person. Another important lesson is never to lose faith and do not become hopeless from the mercy of Allah. Even if a person's sins are equal to the foam of the sea, Allah will forgive them with sincere repentance.

A Newly Converted Muslim

Sheikh Abdul Wahid Bin Zaid (Rah), who was a well-known spiritual leader, narrated a story. He said, "Once, we were sailing in a boat when a storm blew our boat to an island, where we landed and saw a man engaged in idol worship."

We said to him, "Whom do you worship?" And he pointed toward the idol.

We said, "You have moulded your god with your own hands! Our Lord, whom we worship, is the Creator of all things. Hand-made idols are not worthy of worship."

The man asked, "Whom do you worship?"

We replied, "We worship Allah, the sacred Being Whose Throne is above the Heavens, Who controls the world's affairs. Whose majesty and glory transcend everything."

The man said, "How did you come to know Him?"

We said, "Our Lord sent us His Messenger (Muhammad PBUH), who was noble of birth and having the most excellent character. This Prophet (PBUH) taught us all these things."

He said, "Where is that the Prophet (PBUH) now?"

We said, "After conveying the message of his Lord, his obligation was fulfilled, and our Lord called him back to Him so that He might grant him good recompense and reward him for conveying His message completely and properly."

The man said, "Did your Prophet (PBUH) leave behind any signs of his Apostleship (any source of guidance) for you?"

We said, "He left for us the Word of Allah, the Holy Quran."

The man asked to be shown the Book, and we placed the Holy Quran before him.

He said that he did not know how to read and requested us to recite from the Book. We recited a Surah from the Quran, to which he listened with tears falling from his eyes. After reciting it up to the last verse, he said, "It is due from us to Him Who revealed this Book that we should never disobey His commandments."

After this, he accepted Islam, and we taught him the fundamentals of Islam and some of the Commandments of Allah. We also taught him a few Surahs of the Holy Quran. When we were preparing to go to bed at night, after observing 'Isha Prayer', the man said, "Does your Lord also sleep?"

We said, "He is the Alive, the Eternal; Neither slumber nor sleep overtakes Him."

He then said, "How impudent you people are that sleep while your Lord is awake!"

We were amazed at his words. When we were going to leave the island, the man asked us to take him with us, saying that he wished to learn more about the new faith. We took him on board, and our boat sailed back to the city of Abadan, Iran.

On reaching there, I said to my friends, "Let us contribute to our newly converted brother, for he must need money for his provision."

We collected some dirhams and presented the money to him.

He asked, "What is this?" and we told him that it was something to help him in meeting his needs.

He recited, 'La Ilaha lliallaho' and said, "You have shown me a path you are not following yourself. I lived on an island and worshipped an idol instead of worshipping Allah, and still, He did not destroy me nor let me die of hunger, though I did not know Him. How He can destroy me now that I know Him (and worship Him!)."

Three days later, we were told that he was on his deathbed and his last hour had drawn near. We visited him and asked him if he had any wishes. He replied, "He Who sent you to the island for my 'Hidayat' (guidance) has fulfilled all my wishes."

As we sat there, I (Abdul Wahid) dozed off and dreamt that I saw a green and pleasant garden, in which there stood a magnificent domed building. A throne was laid in a room of the building, on which there sat a most beautiful damsel, the like of whom, in beauty, I had never seen before. She was saying, "O, send him to me soon. I beseech you in the name of Allah; I am so fond of him that I cannot bear to be separated from him anymore."

Lesson: These are the miraculous manifestations of Allah's infinite bounty and forgiveness! The man spent most of his life worshipping idols. But when his hour of death drew near, Allah raised a storm to blow a boat to the island. Thus he was granted eternal heavenly bliss through the guidance of the people on board.

An Anonymous Prince

Khalifah Haroon Rashid had a son, about sixteen years of age, who was associated with the ascetics and spiritual leaders of those times. He would often go to the graveyard to think about his mortality.

One day, the young boy came to his father's court (the court of Haroon Rasheed), where his father was sitting in company with lords and noblemen. The boy was dressed in simple clothes. When the courtiers saw him in this condition, they said, "The ways of this boy are a disgrace to our king. If he could scold him, the boy might give up his stupid habits."

Upon hearing this, the Khalifah said to his son, "My dear son, you have disgraced me in people's sight."

The boy did not utter a word (to his father) but called out to a bird sitting nearby, "O bird, I command you, in the name of Him Who created you, to come and sit on my hand." The bird flew across to him and sat on his hand. The boy then commanded it to fly away.

After this, the boy addressed his father, "My dear father, it is your attachment to the world, which is a disgrace to me. I have decided to leave the palace."

The boy went away, taking only a copy of the Holy Quran with him. When he was taking permission from his mother, she gave him a precious ring, which he could sell in need. The boy then went to Basrah and started working as a labourer. He was only working once a week and used his one-day wages for the whole week.

Once a person named Abu Aamir Basri hired him. Abu Aamir then narrated a story of what happened when he hired him.

Abu Amir said:

Once a wall of my house collapsed, and I needed a mason to reconstruct it. Somebody told me about a young boy who was doing masonry work. I looked for him, and there I saw a handsome young boy reciting the Holy Quran.

I asked him if he would be available for the masonry work, and he said, "Surely, we have been created to toil and do some work in our lives."

He said, "I shall take a dirham and a Danaq as my wages for the day. I shall have to halt work for prayer and resume work after the prayer." I agreed to his conditions.

He came and started work on the wall. When I came in the evening, I was surprised to see that he had done a work of almost ten masons. I offered him two dirhams, but he declined and took only a dirham and a Danaq.

The following day, I went out again, looking for him, but found out that he worked only on Saturdays. As I was happy with his work, so I delayed the construction for him until Saturday. On Saturday, I found him in the same place, reciting the Holy Quran. We agreed on the same conditions.

Wondering how he had done ten workers' work last time, I watched him unnoticed. I was surprised when I saw that the stones automatically joined together when he put mortar on the wall. I realised that he was quite near Allah, which was why an unseen power was assisting him. I wanted to give him three dirhams at the end of the work, but he took just a dirham and a Danaq and left, saying, "I have no use for more than this amount."

I waited for him for another week and looked for him again next Saturday but could not find him anywhere. A person told me that he had been ill for a few days. I hired a guide to lead me to his place. When I reached there, I found him lying unconscious on the ground, with his head on a brick.

I greeted him but got no response. I said, 'Assalaam-o-Alaikum' again, a bit louder. This time he opened his eyes and recognised me. I laid his head in my lap, but he moved it back on the piece of brick.

The boy then said, "Abu Amir, when I die, wash me and shroud me in the clothes I am wearing now."

I said, "Oh my Dear, I see no harm in buying new cloth for your shroud."

He said, "The living is more in want of new clothes than the dead."

The boy said, "The shroud will quickly decay, but what remains with a deceased is his deeds. Give my turban and the waste jug to the grave-digger. When you bury me, take this copy of the Holy Quran and this ring to Khalifah Haroon Rashid. Please deliver them into his own hands and say to him with the words, 'O father, take heed and let the death not come to you while you are indulged in the world.'"

The young boy took his last breath with these words on his lips. At that moment, I knew that he was a prince.

After his death, I followed his instructions for the funeral. After the burial, I travelled to Baghdad to deliver the ring and the Holy Book to the Khalifah. When I reached the palace, he was just coming out of the court in his protocol. I stood on a high platform. On seeing him, I called in a loud voice, "O, Ameer-ul-Momineen (king of Muslims), I request you, in the name of your kinship with Muhammad (PBUH), to stop for a moment."

Haroon Rashid stopped and looked around. I moved forward and said, "These things were entrusted to me by a boy who died and requested me that these should be delivered into your own hands."

The Khalifah looked at the ring and the Holy Quran and hung his head in sorrow. I saw tears dripping from his eyes. The king then told his chamberlain to escort me to his palace and present me to him when he returned to the palace. I stayed in the palace until the Khalifah came back in the evening. He ordered the curtains to be drawn down and asked for my presence. He said, "The man will just revive my sorrow."

The chamberlain came to me and said, "The king wants you, but he is shocked. Try to cut it in half if you want to say something."

He then took me into the private room of the Khalifah. He asked me to come closer to him, and when I had taken my seat, he asked, "Do you know my son?"

I said yes. He asked me, "What did he do for a living?" I told him that he did the work of a mason." The Khalifah said, "Did you also hire him to do the work of a mason?" I said yes.

The Khalifah said, "Did it not occur to your mind that he had a kinship with the Prophet Muhammad (PBUH)."

I said, "O Ameer-ul-Momineen! First of all, I beg forgiveness from Allah and then beg your pardon, but I did not know of it. I only learned about him after he had passed away."

The Khalifah said, "Did you wash his body with your own hands?" I said, Yes, and he asked, "Let me touch your hand." He held my hand close to his chest and recited a few verses.

Haroon Rashid decided to go to Basrah to visit his son's grave. I, Abu Aamir, also accompanied him. Standing by his son's grave, he recited a few verses.

The following night, when I went to bed, in my dream, I saw a domed building bathed in light (Noor), above which there hung a cloud of light. Out of this cloud of light came the voice of the deceased boy, talking to me, "Abu Aamir, May Allah grant you the best reward (for washing and shrouding me and fulfilling my will)!"

I asked him, "My dear friend, how are you doing in the next world?" He replied, "My Lord, Who is the most Bounteous One, He granted me such bounties as eyes have never seen, ears have never heard of, and minds have never thought about."

Someone inquired Haroon Rashid about this boy, and he said he was born before the ascension to the Caliphate and was brought up very well. He had learned the Holy Quran and other related branches of religious knowledge, but when I rose to be a king, he left me and went away. The boy was very obedient to his mother.

Lesson: The Prophet Muhammad (PBUH) said, "Allah said, I have prepared for My righteous slaves (such excellent things) as no eye has ever seen, nor an ear has ever heard, nor a human heart can ever think of." This world's happiness is short-lived. Every living being has to leave this world and move to the eternal one. Righteous people always work to achieve happiness in life Hereafter.

From Wrestling to Sainthood

Before sainthood, Hazrat Sheikh Junaid Baghdadi (Rah) worked as a professional wrestler for the king. As usual, one day, the ruler organised an open, challenging competition and announced that anyone who beats the imperial wrestler will be rewarded with a huge amount. Everyone knew Junaid's strengths. A large audience was gathered and was looking forward to the challenger.

Surprisingly, a poor, feeble and skinny person stood up and asked to enter the contest with Junaid. When people saw the challenger, they could not believe their eyes. Everyone thought about how the old man could fight Junaid. The king was among the audience and was bound to allow the challenger as he could not stop someone from entering the bout with free will. The shaky old man was permitted to enter the ring.

Both wrestlers faced each other and started warming up. Just before the start of the match, the challenger whispered in Junaid's ears, "Everyone knows that I cannot beat you. But I am a Sayyid (a descendant of Prophet Muhammad PBUH). We have no food, and my family is starving at home. You work for the king, have money, and have already earned a name. If you lose this competition, then you may lose the money and your honour for the time being. But the prize money I would get by winning will help my family and me for a long time. I beseech you that let me win this contest for the sake of the Prophet's lineage. Are you not willing to sacrifice your honour for the sake of the children of the Prophet (PBUH)?"

Sheikh Junaid was shocked to hear such a request from his rival. They grappled with each other in front of a large audience. Everyone believed that the old man would have to face the worst day of his life. However, down there in the ring, Junaid's heart melted, and he decided to lose the competition. He preferred a disgrace in this world over respect for the family of Prophet Muhammad (PBUH).

In a display of fervour, Junaid demonstrated a few manoeuvres and his finesse so that the king does not suspect any foul play. Junaid, without using force, allowed himself to be dropped. The old man mounted on Junaid's chest and declared his victory. The king could not believe it, but that was the truth that the old skinny person won the prize. The king and crowd insulted and intimidated Junaid for such a shameful performance. When he reached home, his family was also worried about what had happened as he had lost his honour.

Junaid accepted the great disgrace, but his heart was satisfied with what happened. That night when Junaid went to sleep, he saw the Prophet Muhammad (PBUH) in his dream, who said, "O Junaid. You sacrificed your fame for the love of my descendants. Your disgrace will be turned into such an honour that your name and status would be heralded worldwide."

Lesson: Junaid was a wrestler and probably was not known outside his country. But due to his love for the Prophet (PBUH) and his sacrifice, he was transformed into a powerful saint. Even after centuries, people still remember his name with great reverence and respect. He became from the wrestler Junaid to the Great Sheikh Junaid Baghdadi (Rah). This means that a strong belief in one's faith is more powerful than physical strength.

From a Governor to a Beggar

Once king (Khalifa) invited all his governors to his court and rewarded those who performed well. At the end of the meeting, he gifted a robe to every governor. While the king was enjoying his company with the governors, one governor felt the urge to sneeze. He could not control the sneeze, and afterwards, he wiped his nose on the robe of honour. At that time, the king noticed him and became furious. The king scolded him for disrespecting his gifted robe, stripped him of the robe and removed him from his court.

The king was upset by the event and ended the court. After a while, the guards came and asked that the Governor of Demavend, Abu Bakr Al-Shibli of Khorasan, wanted to meet him. The king granted the permission.

When the governor came inside, he asked, "Is sneezing intentional or unintentional?"

The king understood his intention, dodged the question, and told him it had nothing to do with him.

The governor then asked another question, "Do you think that such a punishment for wiping his nose on a gifted rob was really necessary? Could it be justifiable to insult him in court in front of everyone, or could it be less?"

The king warned the governor to stop such questions as he was not accountable to him. Otherwise, he would regret it.

The governor continued, "O king, I understand one thing: that you gifted a gown to a person, and he did not fully respect it. Then you insulted him in front of everyone. I understand now that Allah also bestowed on my body with Islam. If I do not respect his gift, then Allah would also insult me on the Day of Judgement."

He then threw his gown in front of the king and resigned from the governorship to please Allah and avoid devastation on the Day of Judgement.

After this incident, he decided to devote himself to getting the pleasure of Allah. When he came out of the court, he wondered what to do now. Then he thought about Junaid Baghdadi (Rah), a great saint, to learn some spiritual knowledge from him.

He went to Junaid and said, "I heard that you have the gift of knowledge. You can pass it to me for free or for a price if you want."

Junaid said, "I cannot sell it to you because you would not afford it, and if I give you for free, you will not respect it."

Shibli asked, "What should I do?"

Junaid replied, "Let's stay here for some time, and when I see that you are ready, you can start learning it."

After a few months, Junaid asked him, "What do you do?"

He replied. "I was governor of a region."

Junaid ordered him, "Go and be a seller of sulphur in Baghdad for a year."

The smell of sulphur and the job made him very frustrated. After one year, he came back to Junaid.

When Junaid saw him, he ordered, "Oh, so you were counting days. Go and run the shop for another year." Shibli went back.

Now Shibli forgot about the time and focused on the work. One day, Junaid asked him, "Have you completed the year?"

He said, "I do not know."

Junaid asked to go and start begging in Baghdad.

Shibli was surprised to hear that but obeyed his teacher and spent a year begging on the streets of Baghdad without success. He returned to Junaid after a year. The master tried to remove arrogance and pride from his heart, and the whole exercise was a part of spiritual education.

One day Junaid asked him, "What is your name?"

"Shibli", he replied. Now he was not calling himself governor.

After three years of hard work, he was allowed to start learning spiritualism. In a short period, he learned so much that his heart was full of Allah's love.

At last, Junaid called him and said, "When you were governor of a province, you may have done something wrong to the people. So you should prepare a list of the people who were victims of your injustice when you were governor. You would not clean the inners unless your dealings with people are not straight."

When the list was ready, Junaid told him, "Return now to the province and find every person on the list. Apologise to them. And let them forgive you for whatever you did to them."

Some people forgave him while others put conditions. After two years, he returned to Junaid. It was almost five years under Junaid's education. At last, he became a great saint.

Lesson: We should understand Allah's happiness and annoyance. He blessed us with so many things, such as our body, family, house, etc. We should thank God for all these blessings. The real thankfulness will come out from our hearts when we remove bad feelings and arrogance.

The other lesson was about respect for the teacher. Despite the fact Shibli was from a wealthy family and governed the whole province, he was a beggar for one year. Shibli could tell Junaid that he did not want to do begging or other trivial jobs, but he obeyed his teacher.

Bahlool and the Great Saint

Bahlool was born in Iraq, and his real name was Wahab bin Amr. He lived in the time of King Harun al-Rashid. Bahlool was a well-known judge and scholar who came from a wealthy background and belonged to the king's (Caliph) family. He acted insanely on his teacher's order to be saved from Harun's punishment. In reality, Bahlool was a saint and sage. At that time, another great saint and an Islamic scholar lived there.

One day, the Great Sheikh[20] went for a walk in Baghdad with his disciples. The Great Sheikh inquired about Bahlool and asked to look for him. Eventually, they found Bahlool in a desert, sleeping on the ground with his head on a stone.

When the Sheikh reached near him, he saw Bahlool in a state of perturbation.

The Sheikh greeted him with Salaam.

Bahlool answered and asked, "Who are you?"

"The Great Sheikh introduced himself."

Bahlool asked, "I heard you give people spiritual education?"

The Sheikh replied meekly with yes.

Bahlool asked, "Do you even know how to eat?"

The Sheikh then said, "Yes, I know. I first say Bismillah (In the Name of Allah). I eat from in front of me; I take small bites, put them in my mouth's right side, and slowly chew. I do not stare at others' bites. While eating, I remember Allah. For whatever morsel I eat, I say Alhamdolillah (Praise be to Allah). I wash my hands before and after eating."

Bahlool stood up, brushed off his shirt and said, "You want to be the spiritual teacher of the world, but you even don't even know how to eat." Saying this, he walked away.

One of the Sheikh's disciples angrily said, "O Sheikh! He is an eccentric person. Do not worry about what he just said to you."

The Sheikh shook his head and said, "He may be a lunatic, but he is better than thousand intelligent people. He knows the truth. Let's go after him. We have to learn from him."

Saying this, he went after Bahlool, and his disciples also followed him.

They did not call Bahlool but kept following until he reached a deserted site and sat down. The Sheikh came near him and repeated Salaam.

Bahlool looked at him and asked, "Who are you?"

The Sheikh introduced himself again.

"Oh! The Sheikh who does not even know how to eat," Bahlool said.

He confessed, "Yes, I am the Sheikh who doesn't know how to eat."

Bahlool asked indifferently, "You don't know how to eat, but do you know how to talk?"

The Sheikh replied, "Yes."

Bahlool asked him, "How do you talk?"

This time, the Sheikh tried to cover as much as possible. "I talk in moderation and to the point. I do not speak unnecessarily and without purpose. I speak according to the knowledge of the audience so they can understand. I call the people towards Allah and the Prophet (AS). I do not talk excessively that people would get bored. I care about the deepness of inner and outer knowledge."

Behlool raged, "What sort of person you are. Forget about eating; you even don't know how to talk either." Bahlool stood up in displeasure, dusted his dress on the Sheikh and walked away.

The angry disciples said, "O Sheikh! You have seen that he is a disrespectful and crazy person. He does not know your status and is unaware of your knowledge. Just leave him alone, and let's go out from here."

The Sheikh replied, "No! He is full of wisdom; I need him. Let's come with me."

Again he went after Bahlool until he reached near him.

Bahlool looked back and asked, "O Sheikh! What do you want from me? You do not know how to eat, and neither do you know the manners of speaking. Perhaps you also do not know how to sleep?"

The Sheikh replied, "I know. I can tell you that."

Bahlool sat down on the ground and said, "Ok, tell me then, how do you sleep?"

The Sheikh also sat on the ground and explained, "When I am finished with Salat-e-Isha (Isha prayer) and reciting supplications, I put on my sleepwear. I follow all the Islamic manners of sleeping transmitted to us by our elders."

Bahlool said, "I am surprised that you do not know how to sleep either." He wanted to get up, but the Great Sheikh held his garment and said, "O Dear Bahlool! I don't know anything, so for the sake of Allah, teach me."

Bahlool smiled and said, "Before you claimed knowledge and said you knew, so I was avoiding you. Now that you confessed your lack of knowledge, I will teach you. Then listen."

The Sheikh said, "I am ready to learn."

Bahlool said, "What you described about the eating were secondary. The truth behind eating meals is that you eat halal (lawful) morsels. If you eat haram (forbidden) food likewise, with one hundred manners, it won't benefit you but will be the reason for blackening the heart."

The Sheikh said, "May Allah grant you a glorious reward. You opened my eyes."

Bahlool continued, "When it comes to talking, the first thing is that your heart must be clean and have good intentions before you begin to talk. And your conversation must be to please Allah. If it is for any worldly or useless work, it will become a calamity for you, no matter how you express yourself. That is why silence would be best.

"Whatever you said about sleeping is also of secondary importance. The truth of it is that your heart should be free of enmity, jealousy, and hate. Your heart should not be greedy for this world or its wealth and remember Allah when going to sleep."

The Sheikh kissed Bahlool's hand and prayed for him. The disciples who considered Bahlool a crazy person felt ashamed and started using the new lessons in their lives.

Lesson: One of the important lessons is no matter how educated and well learned a person is, there is always someone more learned out there. If a person doesn't know something, he shouldn't be ashamed of learning it. Despite the Great Sheikh being one of the most learned people on earth at his time but he felt no shame in learning from another person.

Burn Your Boats

Tariq bin Ziyad was a Muslim general who led the Islamic conquest of Visigothic Hispania in 711-718 AD. Tariq bin Ziyad was a new convert to Islam from the Berber tribe of Algeria. He was said to be a freed slave. He is considered to be one of the most important military commanders in Iberian history. Under the orders of the Umayyad Caliph Al-Walid I, he led an army from the north coast of Morocco, consolidating his troops on a large hill now known as Gibraltar. The name "Gibraltar" is the Spanish derivation of the Arabic name "Jabal Tariq", meaning "mountain of Tariq", named after him.

It is said that he saw the Holy Prophet (PBUH) in his dream, who was saying: "Take courage, O Tariq! And accomplish what you are destined to perform." Then he saw Muhammad (PBUH) and his Companions (RA) entering Andalus. From that moment, he never doubted his victory.

He led a small force from Morocco in 711 AD and landed on the high rock (Gibraltar) with an army of 12,000 men, mostly Berbers, Syrians, and Yemenis. He was to face King Roderic of Spain, who assembled six times more men to his back (some history book states that he amassed a force of 100,000 fighters against the Muslims).

When Tariq bin Ziyad found the Muslim ranks a bit nervous in the face of the large enemy in front of them, he ordered the ships to be burned. After he burned his own boats, taking away any route to escape for his army, he then delivered the historic and stirring address to his army for incitement, forcing himself and his men to either succeed or die.

He said, "O my warriors, whether would you flee? Behind you is the sea, before you, the enemy. You have left now only the hope of your courage and your constancy."

The two armies met on the battlefield of Guadalete, where King Roderic was defeated and killed.

He then defeated the Spanish army, which retreated toward Toledo. Tariq bin Ziyad divided his troops into four regiments for a hot pursuit. One regiment advanced toward Cordoba and subdued the enemy. The second captured Murcia while the third advanced toward Saragossa. Tariq himself moved swiftly toward Toledo. The city surrendered without resistance, and with that, King Roderic's rule came to an end in Spain.

Commander Musa bin Nusair then joined Tariq bin Ziyad. The two generals occupied more than two-thirds of the Iberian Peninsula (Spain and Portugal and a small area of Southern France, Andorra and Gibraltar). Spain remained under Muslim rule for more than 750 years, from 711 to 1492.

Lesson: For Tariq, it was all or nothing. Failure was not an option, and he forced himself and his men to either succeed or die.

A retreat is easy when it is an option. People flee in fear and postpone all important actions until the fear dissipates. The story teaches us to act decisively despite fear. We also ask ourselves, what are our ships? What am I afraid of to let go?

A Teenage Army General

Muhammad bin Qasim was an Arab military commander who led the Muslim conquest of Sindh (now part of Pakistan) and defeated Raja Dahir, the last ruler of the Brahman dynasty of Sindh, in the battle of Aror. He was the first Muslim to capture Hindu territories successfully and initiated early Islamic India in 712 AD. Qasim was orphaned as a child and was brought up by his mother. His uncle, Hajjaj bin Yousaf (famous for his brutality), taught him the art of governing and warfare. Qasim's abilities as a general became apparent when he became the commander to invade Sindh at the age of seventeen. He was also an excellent administrator and a kind-hearted and religious person.

The Muslims did their best to be friendly with the Raja (king) of Sindh. But there was little response from the other side. When Dahir became Raja, he got more active in creating troubles for Muslims. Hindu rebels once attacked Muslim ships travelling from Sri Lanka to Saudi Arabia through the sea routes of Sindh and took away their possessions while keeping Muslim men and women as prisoners with them.

An Arab girl was kidnapped during the attack and was imprisoned. However, she escaped from prison and informed the Muslim governor about the attack on the ship.

She also pleaded for help by writing a letter to Hajjaj, the powerful governor at that time.

Hajjaj wrote a letter to Raja Dahir to release the prisoners as soon as possible. The Hindu Raja was extremely kind to the rebels and pirates. He replied to Hajjaj that he had no control over the rebels. This was an act of open enmity toward the Muslims.

Hajjaj then decided to take action against the attackers. He asked Muhammad bin Qasim to attack India. Qasim departed with 6,000 Syrian cavalry and 6,000 camel riders. They first attacked Debal (a port in Sindh), a strong fortress and fully protected by solid fortifications. There was a temple Hindus believed that the idol god alone was enough to beat back any enemy attacks.

The fortress was placed under siege by the Muslims. Hindu spirits remained high as they thought no one could take the fortress by force. At last, Qasim found the real secret of Hindu morale. A Brahman in the area told Qasim that the fortress could not be captured unless something was done about the talisman prepared by the Brahmans.

"What talisman?" asked Qasim in surprise.

Brahman replied, "You see the forty-yard high steeple of the temple and the great red flag flying from it. At the base of the flagstaff, the Brahmans have placed a talisman. No harm can come to the town as long as the flag is there."

Qasim now knew the secret that the Hindu spirits would remain high as long as the red flag was intact. He must do something about the flag. It was not very difficult to smash the flag. Qasim ordered the artillery to make the flagstaff the target and brought out his best catapult (Manjanik), also called the "Bride", and positioned it across the massive temple. The third stone struck it and shattered its base. The talisman was broken, and the great red flag was annihilated.

When the people of Debal saw their revered holy flag and the flagstaff fall, their hearts sank, and they lost their courage and will to fight at this bad omen. Qasim seized the opportunity and ordered his troops to storm the fort from different directions. At last, the Hindus were defeated. Qasim was tolerant and treated the Hindus kindly. Their temple was left untouched, and priests were left alone. The Hindu governor of the town begged for mercy and was allowed to continue as governor. Before leaving Debal, Qasim laid out a Muslim quarter in the town. Here he built the first-ever mosque on the Hindus' land.

But even after the fall of Debal, there was no trace of Raja Dahir and his army. Qasim ordered to teach this vain Raja a lesson. The fall of Debal made Dahir furious, and he was trying to scare Qasim of consequences by sending him threatening letters. Qasim was on the hunt for Dahir for months and conquered other cities on his way.

At last, both armies faced each other. On June 20, 712 AD, Dahir mounted on his elephant and ordered the attack. Dahir seemed really desperate and fought like a wildcat. At last, an arrow struck him, and he fell from his elephant. But he managed to mount on a horse, and the fighting re-started with full fury. Just as the sun was going down, he was killed by an Arab soldier. When Hindus saw him dead, they lost their heart and fled from the field. Qasim won a complete victory.

Hajjaj tried to uproot idolatry from Sindh, though he also stressed public wellbeing. In a letter to Qasim, he wrote, "Treat them kindly. Try to win them over. Try to promote their wellbeing. If those who took up arms against you seek refuge, do not hesitate to forgive them. Keep your promise so that people know you can be trusted. If you once go back on your word, you will lose respect. People will stop trusting you."

The conquest that started on a plea of a woman resulted in being fruitful for Arab Muslims. A lot of resources were utilised to attack India, yet all was done on a single call of help from a woman. Qasim, however, died at the young age of 20.

Lesson: Qasim was extraordinarily kind and sympathetic and did his utmost to make the people happy. By his kind treatment, he won the hearts of the people. Such kindness in rulers was a thing unknown in Sindh. He was as kind-hearted and tolerant as ever. He made it known to the people that those who laid down arms would be forgiven. Many took advantage of this offer. When idolaters saw his kindness, they started embracing Islam. The young general of Islam knew how to conquer men's hearts. This proved a more powerful weapon than the sword.

Sheikh Kharaqani and the Sultan

During the reign of Sultan Mahmud Ghaznavi, Sheikh Abu Al-Hassan Kharaqani (Rah) was a very famous saint. Sheikh Kharaqani was one of the master Sufis of Islam. However, he was illiterate but had wide inspirational knowledge about the Quran and Hadith.

Sultan became very eager to see Sheikh Kharaqani and travelled from Ghazni to Kharaqan. Given that he was the ruler, he sent his messenger to Sheikh Kharaqani to inform him, "The Sultan had travelled all that long to see you. He would be glad if you visit his palace." Sultan told his messenger that if Abu Al-Hassan refused for visiting, then recite this verse of the Quran[21], "O believers! Obey Allah and obey the Messenger and those in authority among you."

When the messenger reached the Sheikh and conveyed the Sultan's message, he excused himself and refused to visit him. Then the messenger recited the verse of the Quran that which Sultan mentioned. The verse stressed obeying God, Prophet (PBUH) and the ruler.

The Sheikh replied to the messenger, "I am so busy following the God commandments that I am so shameful when it comes to my beloved Prophet (PBUH), so how can I spare time to get attention to the ruler."

The messenger went back to Sultan and informed him about the Sheikh's answer. When Sultan heard the answer, he was impressed and visited him by himself. He requested the Sheikh to tell about Hazrat Bayazid Bastami. Sheikh told Sultan that Bayazid said, "Whoever saw me he would be saved from infidelity and polytheism."

Sultan replied that at the time of Muhammad (PBUH), there were so many infidels and wretched people such as Abu Jahl and Abu Lahab, but they died as non-Muslims. Does that mean Bayazid's rank was higher than that of Muhammad (PBUH)?

Upon hearing this, Sheikh Kharaqani's face was flushed, and he roared, "Mahmud, do not cross the line of respect. Muhammad (PBUH) was only seen by his Companions (RA), whereas infidels, in fact, did not see Muhammad (PBUH)." He recited the verse of the Quran[22]:

"And you see them looking at you, yet they do not see."

Sultan was very impressed after talking to the Sheikh, and in the end, he asked for advice. The Sheikh told him to take care of four things:

- Avoid things that God has prohibited for us;
- Pray in the congregation;
- Be generous;
- Be kind and merciful to people.

Sultan then asked for benediction. The Sheikh raised his hands and said, "May Allah forgive all the true Muslims."

Sultan asked to make a special prayer for him. The Sheikh prayed for him and said, "May Allah be merciful to you and give you a better place in the Hereafter."

Afterwards, Sultan presented a sack of gold coins and asked Sheikh to accept this small gift. The Sheikh looked at Sultan in great surprise, and then he offered barley bread to Sultan and asked him to eat. Sultan started with Bismillah, but the first loaf was stuck in his throat.

Sheikh asked whether the loaf was stuck in the throat. Sultan nodded. Sheikh then replied, "The sack of the gold coin is also stuck in my throat. You should take it back quickly. These coins are the food of kings, and for saints (Faquir), barley bread is a great blessing."

Sultan insisted he take some coins, and by which the Shiekh said in his glorious voice, "I left the materialistic world, and I divorced this world and made the gold coins haram on myself. You must not insist on this. Even you have no right on these as they belong to the people. If you distribute it against the will of the people, then that would be dishonesty, and that would be a big sin in front of Allah."

He continued, "If you want to donate these coins, then the country is full of poor people who seem prosperous, but they cannot spread their hands to others due to self-respect. You will be accountable for these people on the Day of Judgement. You have to answer why you did not take care of them during your rule."

These words shook the Sultan, and tears started from his eyes. He then said to the Sheikh, if you are not taking anything from me, why not give me some consecrated things? The Sheikh quickly removed his shirt and gave it to the Sultan.

When Sultan asked permission to leave, the Sheikh stood for his respect. The Sultan became surprised and asked, "Why do you stand up for farewell? You did not give me much attention and respect when I arrived."

The Sheikh replied, "When you came to my place, you behaved like a king and tried to show off your status; that is why I did not care about King Mahmud. But now, on leaving, you are a changed person and departing like a humble and pious person. Therefore, I consider it my responsibility to stand in your respect. A true Muslim should respect such a humble person."

Moral: If a person is on the right path and follows Allah's commandments. Allah gives that person so much respect that even kings start respecting them. Sultan Mahmud was a great king of his time, but he travelled to a fakir (saint) to get his blessings. He gave up all his kingly traits after meeting the pious person.

Bibliography

101 Sabaq Amoz Waqiat By Maulana Haroon Muawiyah

Ahl E Dil Kay Tarpa Denay Walay By Maulana Zulfiqar Ahmad Naqshbandi

Ashraful Adab Sharah Nafhatul Arab By Maulana Abdul Hafeez

Bahishti Zewar By Ashraf Ali Thanwi

Bikhre Moti By Shaykh Muhammad Yunus Palanpuri

Bosathan By Sheikh Saadi

Dilchasp Anokhy Waqiat By Maulana Arsalan bin Akhtar

Fazail E Sadaqat By Muhammad Zakariya

Hayat ul Haiwan By Allama Kamal-ud-Din Al-Dameeri

Hikayat-e-Saadi By Sheikh Saadi

Hikayat-E-Sahaba By Maulana Muhammad Zakariyya

Hikayat-e-Sufiya By Talib Al-Hashmi

Imam Abu Hanifa Kay Hairat Angaiz Waqiaat By Maulana Abdul Qayyum Haqqani

Khair-ul-Majaalis By Hazrat Khwaja Naseeruddin Chiragh Dehlavi Chishti

Maariful Quran By Mufti Muhammad Shafi

Makhzan e Akhlaq By Maulana Rehmatullah Subhani

Manaqib Al Imam Al Azam Abu Hanifa By Al Moufiq Bin Ahmed Al Maki

Maut Ka Manzar Marne Ke Baad Kya Hoga By Khwaja
Mohammed Islam

Nuzhat Al-Majaalis By Sheikh Abdur-Rahmaan ibn Abdus-
Salaam as-Saffoori

Safarnama Ibn-e-Batuta Urdu By Ibn Battuta

Sahih al-Bukhari By Muhammad ibn Ismail al-Bukhari

Sahih Muslim By Muslim ibn al-Hajjaj

Tafsir ibn Kathir By Ibn Kathir

Talbis Iblis By Imam Ibn Jawzi

Tanbihul Ghafilin By Nasr ibn Muhammad Abu al-Layth al-
Samarqandi

Tarikh-i Tabari By Muhammad ibn Jarir al-Tabari

Tazkirat al-Awliya By Farid al-Din Attar

Notes

---

[1] Rah stands for Rahmat Ullah Alaih, which means Allah's mercy is upon him..

[2] Abu Hanifa Al-Numan Ibn Thabit commonly known as Imam Abu Hanifa was an 8th century Sunni Muslim theologian and jurist who became the eponymous founder of the Hanafi school of Sunni jurisprudence. He is also known as al-Imam al-Azam (The Greatest Imam).

[3] A minbar is a pulpit in a mosque where the imam stands to deliver sermons.

[4] Hazrat is a common title used to honour a person.

[5] Hadith means record of the traditions or sayings of the Prophet Muhammad (PBUH).

[6] The word nafs (ego/soul) in the context of human speech shows a side in human that has good and bad potential.

[7] Halal is an Arabic term which means permissible or lawful in Islam

[8] Sufi (saint) practices Sufism (Tasawwuf), which is mystical Islamic belief and practice in which Muslims seek to find the truth of divine love and knowledge through direct personal experience of God.

[9] Sulaiman (Solomon) was the son of Prophet Dawud (David).

[10] AS stands for alayhi s-salam, which means Peace Be Upon Him. This is used for prophets

[11] PBUH stands for Peace be upon him. It is a phrase used to pay respect to the Prophet Muhammad (PBUH) or any other prophets believed to be sent by Allah.

[12] RA stands for Arabic phrase Radi Allahu Anhu which means May Allah be pleased with him. When there are more than one companion, it is called Radiya llahu an-hum which means May Allāh be pleased with them.

[13] [Sahih Bukhari: 5735]

[14] Amir-ul-Momineen is an Arabic title designating the supreme leader or king of an Islamic country.

[15] Prophet Ibrahim (AS) is also known as Prophet Abraham in the Hebrew Bible.

[16] [Quran (4:125)]

[17] To be a companion, it required the criterion of meeting the Prophet Muhammad (PBUH) while having faith, and died as a Muslim.

[18] Also spelled Osman, was the third Rashidun caliph. The Rashidun Caliphs are the first four caliphs who led the Muslim community following the death of the Islamic prophet Muhammad: Abu Bakr (RA), Umar (RA), Uthman (R), and Ali (RA).

[19] The Prophet Musa Ibn Imran known as Prophet Moses (AS) in the Bible, considered a prophet and messenger in Islam.

[20] The story of Junaid and Behlool is cited in several authentic books. However, the author's research shows some unexplainable discrepancy in time period of both saints. Junaid was born in 830 AD but Behlool died around 810 AD. On that basis the author used the Great Saint rather than Junaid Baghdadi.

[21] [Quran (4:59)]

[22] [Quran (7:198)]